Th

A Freshly Baked Cozy Mystery, book 3
by
Kate Bell
Kathleen Suzette

Books by Kathleen Suzette:

A Rainey Daye Cozy Mystery Series

Pumpkin Spice Donuts and a Murder
A Rainey Daye Cozy Mystery, book 14

A Pumpkin Hollow Mystery Series

Candy Coated Murder
A Pumpkin Hollow Mystery, book 1
Murderously Sweet
A Pumpkin Hollow Mystery, book 2
Chocolate Covered Murder
A Pumpkin Hollow Mystery, book 3
Death and Sweets
A Pumpkin Hollow Mystery, book 4
Sugared Demise
A Pumpkin Hollow Mystery, book 5
Confectionately Dead
A Pumpkin Hollow Mystery, book 6
Hard Candy and a Killer
A Pumpkin Hollow Mystery, book 7
Candy Kisses and a Killer
A Pumpkin Hollow Mystery, book 8
Terminal Taffy
A Pumpkin Hollow Mystery, book 9
Fudgy Fatality
A Pumpkin Hollow Mystery, book 10
Truffled Murder
A Pumpkin Hollow Mystery, book 11
Caramel Murder
A Pumpkin Hollow Mystery, book 12
Peppermint Fudge Killer
A Pumpkin Hollow Mystery, book 13

Chocolate Heart Killer
A Pumpkin Hollow Mystery, book 14
Strawberry Creams and Death
A Pumpkin Hollow Mystery, book 15
Pumpkin Spice Lies
A Pumpkin Hollow Mystery, book 16

A Freshly Baked Cozy Mystery Series

Apple Pie A La Murder,
A Freshly Baked Cozy Mystery, Book 1
Trick or Treat and Murder,
A Freshly Baked Cozy Mystery, Book 2
Thankfully Dead
A Freshly Baked Cozy Mystery, Book 3
Candy Cane Killer
A Freshly Baked Cozy Mystery, Book 4
Ice Cold Murder
A Freshly Baked Cozy Mystery, Book 5
Love is Murder
A Freshly Baked Cozy Mystery, Book 6
Strawberry Surprise Killer
A Freshly Baked Cozy Mystery, Book 7
Plum Dead
A Freshly Baked Cozy Mystery, book 8
Red, White, and Blue Murder
A Freshly Baked Cozy Mystery, book 9
Mummy Pie Murder
A Freshly Baked Cozy Mystery, book 10

A Gracie Williams Mystery Series

Pushing Up Daisies in Arizona,

A Gracie Williams Mystery, Book 1
Kicked the Bucket in Arizona,
A Gracie Williams Mystery, Book 2

A Home Economics Mystery Series

Appliqued to Death
A Home Economics Mystery, book 1

Table of Contents

Chapter One

"EXACTLY HOW MANY PIES did you bake?" Alec asked as I handed him two more. I was glad Alec had an SUV. It came in handy when I had a lot of pies to transport. My Toyota just wasn't cutting it.

"Just two more," I assured him. Some people were such worrywarts.

It was Thanksgiving morning, and we were headed to the annual Turkey Trot where we would run a 5K in the frigid cold morning air and then indulge in a piece of pie as a reward. Running had become more and more important to me, and the Turkey Trot had turned into a tradition for me. I was thrilled I would have someone else to run with me this year.

"Are you sure we've got them all?" he asked when I handed him the last of them.

"Yes, that's it," I said. I grabbed my running jacket off the hanger in the hall closet and followed after him. I had baked ten pies for the Turkey Trot and five for our Thanksgiving dinner. I was a little tired, but some caffeine would take care of that.

"Hey, Mom, I'm going to come with you," my son, Thad, mumbled from behind me.

I turned around, surprised to see him up and about. He was dressed in running clothes, with a tuft of blond hair sticking up in the back. He and his girlfriend had flown in late the night before, and I hadn't expected to see him up so early. I smiled at him.

"Okay, honey, come on out, and I'll introduce you to Alec." I was a little nervous about my son meeting my new boyfriend. The word boyfriend even made me nervous. Wasn't I too old to have a boyfriend?

Introductions went around, and we got into Alec's SUV, with Thad in the back. I was glad that Thad was easy going like his father. He wouldn't give me a hard time about dating Alec. It had been eight years since his father had died, and he actually seemed happy that I had met someone.

I was so excited to have Thad home for the holiday that it took all the self-control I had not to nag him about transferring to the University of Maine so I could see him regularly. He was an adult, and I kept reminding myself that he had to make his own decisions.

"Wow, it's chilly out here," I said, buckling my seatbelt. It had been getting increasingly colder in the early mornings, but today was the coldest by far. A light powder snow had fallen in the night, but it would melt as soon as the sun came up.

"It feels colder here for some reason," Thad mumbled, still trying to shake the sleep off.

"It's all that coastal air," Alec said.

"Yeah, I guess I miss that. Or I maybe I don't," Thad said. "I don't mind drier air."

Alec pulled up to the Rec Center ten minutes later, and we got out to unload the pies.

"Hi folks, how are you all doing?" Todd Spellman asked as I picked up an apple pie. Todd was the manager of the local branch of the Bank of Maine. He was pushing his father in a wheelchair. The elder Mr. Spellman wore a wool cap with earflaps, a heavy jacket, and a blanket draped over his legs.

"Good morning, Todd. Good morning, Mr. Spellman," I said, nodding at them. "I'm doing great. Cold, but great."

"It's a fine morning for a run, isn't it?" Todd asked and then glanced at Thad. "Is this your son?"

"Yes, this is Thad," I said. "It's a bit cold for my tastes. I was hoping the weather would turn mild like last year."

Alec came around and stood beside me, and I introduced everyone. Mr. Spellman briefly looked in my direction and then stared off into space. I wasn't quite sure what was ailing him, but it seemed he rarely engaged in conversation anymore.

"Are you going to run, Alec? Thad?" Todd asked. Todd had an all-American charm about him, and I didn't think he had ever met a stranger. It was sweet that he took care of his father in his failing health. He was a young thirty-something, and I didn't think there were many people that age who would devote so much time to an ailing parent.

"Yes, we are. I expect to work up an appetite for that turkey dinner Allie is going to make later this evening," Alec answered.

"That's an excellent plan," Todd said and flashed a perfect movie star smile. "I know Allie is quite the cook."

"Thanks, Todd. Well, we better get the pies inside," I said. I knew Lucy would need help to get set up. "We'll see you out on the course. Mr. Spellman, you save your appetite for some of my pecan pie, you hear? It's the best in the state."

Mr. Spellman looked at me with his eyes glazed over but didn't respond.

"He certainly will," Todd said, patting his father on the shoulder. "I need to get him out of the cold." He turned the wheelchair around and pushed him into the Rec Center building.

"They seem like nice people," Alec said as he reached for two pies.

"Some of the best in town," I said, and picked up another pie. I handed them off to Thad and sent him inside with them, and got two more to take inside. The dry leaves crunched beneath my feet as I headed for the building.

"Oh, Allie, I'm not sure about all of this," Lucy said as I entered the building. She frowned and looked around the room helplessly.

"Not sure about what?" I asked, heading for a table to set my pies down. There were already six other pies there. From the looks of it, three pumpkin, two store-bought apple pies, and someone's attempt at pecan. I didn't want to criticize, but there weren't nearly enough pecans in it.

"This whole thing!" Lucy wailed, motioning toward the empty tables and chairs. A few people milled about with coffee cups in hand, visiting with one another.

"You've got tables and chairs set up, coffee and tea made, and all the forks, spoons, plates, and napkins set out. You even put fall-themed tablecloths on the tables, and have a fire started in the fireplace," I pointed out. "It looks pretty perfect to me. What's upsetting you?"

Lucy Gray was my best friend. She was one of the first people I had met when I moved to Maine over twenty years ago, after marrying my husband, Thaddeus. I don't know how I would have survived the death of my husband without Lucy. But, she could be a little high strung under pressure. Her blond curly hair was sticking out at the sides, and her eyes darted around the room.

"Oh, Ed started the fire." She leaned against a table and crossed her arms. "Diana would have done it so much better. She would have had all sorts of decorations for this event. Look at the bare walls. It seems so empty in here."

"We'll get the rest of the pies," Alec said, heading out the door with Thad. The guys weren't particularly brave around wailing women.

"Now, look. Everyone knows you're doing this on short notice. Everything looks very nice. We are going to have a nice run, and then eat some pie and visit for a bit, then go home and make Thanksgiving dinner. It will be a fun day. You watch and see."

"Do you think so?" she asked, sounding unsure.

Lucy had never hosted a community event, and she never would have if her boss and friend hadn't been murdered last month. Diana Bowen had been the community organizing queen when it came to any kind of event. She lived for them. But she had been poisoned the day of the Halloween bazaar, and that had left the community without an organizer. Lucy had done a great job stepping up with so little notice, even if she didn't feel confident about it.

"Of course," I said and gave her a quick hug as Alec and Thad brought more pies in.

"I'm glad you brought so many pies. I don't know what I'd do if I had been expected to make pies, too," she said.

The annual Turkey Trot brought out a large gathering each year. Many people walked the course, and some just came to visit and eat free pie. It was a fun event that brought the community together.

Ellen Allen came through the door, and I saw Lucy stiffen. "Just take it easy," I told her. Ellen was Lucy's former co-worker who had been fired for stealing from the cash register. The two weren't fond of each other.

It was still dark out as more people began arriving. I grabbed a Styrofoam cup and poured myself some coffee from the huge, industrialized-sized coffee pot.

"Hi, Lucy, the place looks great," Todd Spellman said. "You did a great job pulling this thing together on such short notice."

"Do you think so?" Lucy asked, turning toward him.

"Absolutely! Community involvement is important. If it weren't for people like you and Diana Bowen, God rest her soul, we'd be lost," he said, cheerfully.

I glanced up and saw that Mr. Spellman had been parked near the fireplace. I fixed up the cup of coffee I had poured for myself to give to him instead. I didn't know how he took it, but I decided at this point, he probably didn't either. I put cream and sugar in it and took it to him.

"Here you go, Mr. Spellman," I said loudly in case his hearing wasn't very good. "I brought you some coffee. It's hot, so you need to be careful."

Mr. Spellman turned his head to look at me. I mean, he *really* looked at me. He opened his mouth, but nothing came out. He looked at me so intently, it felt odd. Maybe he had moments of clarity, and he wanted to communicate something to me.

"How are you doing, Mr. Spellman?" I asked, squatting beside his wheelchair. I put the coffee cup in his hands, placing both of them around the cup.

Mr. Spellman shifted the cup to one hand and suddenly grabbed my hand with the other. The movement startled me, and I jumped a little, but I let him hold my hand. He held the coffee cup in his other hand, and it shook a little. His eyes got big, and he squeezed my hand.

"How are you, Mr. Spellman?" I asked again, looking into his eyes. *Was he okay?*

He opened his mouth again, but no sound came out. The intensity of his gaze gave me pause.

"Hey, how's it going?" Todd said, coming up behind me. Mr. Spellman looked up at his son, and Todd gazed back at him. I felt something pass between Todd and his father, but I couldn't put my finger on what it was. "Oh, I see you brought Dad some coffee. Thank you. That's very nice of you," he said. "Are you warm enough, Dad?" He bent and rearranged the blanket on his father's legs.

Mr. Spellman gazed off into the distance and didn't answer.

I stood up. Maybe I was just tired and was imagining things. I had gotten up early to get the pies ready to bring down here, and I still had a race ahead of me. Not that it mattered if I ran fast, or whether I ran at all today. The point was to have fun.

I looked around the room. Thad was in the middle of a group of college-aged kids, laughing. Thad had gone to high school with most of them.

I glanced back at Mr. Spellman. "Enjoy your coffee, Mr. Spellman," I said. "I'll see you out on the course, Todd."

"Indeed, you will," he said brightly.

I headed back over to Alec and Lucy.

"I've got all the pies in," Alec announced as I approached them.

"That's awesome. Thanks," I said, and glanced back at Mr. Spellman.

More people were streaming through the doors. Some brought more pies, and some brought carafes of flavored coffees. The room felt and smelled warm and cozy from the coffee and the fire. It was fall in Maine, and we were going to have a race!

Chapter Two

"ON YOUR MARK, GET SET, go!" came the command from the loudspeaker.

And we were off. Alec started us off at a nice easy pace, but when I saw Todd, Thad, and the group of college kids take off at lightning speed, I was champing at the bit. Something about seeing people running out in front of me made me competitive.

"What are you doing?" Alec asked, increasing his pace to keep up with me.

"Come on, Alec, it's a race! Let's run!" I said breathlessly and pushed myself to go faster.

"You need to pace yourself," he said, still keeping up with me.

"It's only a 5K. What's to pace?" I said. Actually, with the cold air, I was beginning to feel that pace in my lungs, but I wasn't going to let on. "I can do a 5K in my sleep."

"Okay, but don't cry to me when you run out of steam before it's over," he warned.

"Haha," I said. "I'm pretty sure I'll be okay."

"Of course you will be," he said.

I noted the sarcasm, but the cold was making it hard to talk, so I didn't reply.

The trail wound out through the woods and would circle around and come back to the Rec Center. The trees had lost most of their leaves, but some still had a few. The trail had been blown clear of leaves, twigs, and assorted debris and was nice and smooth.

Soon enough I was going to have to switch to treadmill running. The snow could be brutal in Maine in the wintertime, and only the foolhardy would run in it when the weather got nasty.

Much of the early morning powder snow had melted, and I slipped a little on the trail, but caught myself in time, using my arms to balance myself.

"Careful," Alec warned, reaching out for my arm.

"Got it," I answered. A little melting snow wasn't going to hold me back.

It was biting cold, but it was exhilarating, and a nice change from the regular running path. The pine trees were beautiful with a little of the powder snow still stuck on their branches.

Thad and the rest of the college kids were out of sight within a minute or two, and Todd was a hundred yards ahead, giving it his all to try to catch up with them. Poor Todd wasn't going to get anywhere near them. Those kids looked like they were serious athletes. Thad had been a track star in high school, and he was on his college track team.

"How are you doing?" Alec huffed after a couple more minutes.

"Okay, you?" I asked.

He shrugged. "Okay."

We were running hard, and the cold wasn't making it easy. My eyes began to tear up in the cold, and I pulled my scarf further up on my face. I should have worn goggles, but I completely forgot about them.

We went around a curve, and I heard a low whistling sound, and then Todd fell to the ground, face first. He lay still. Alec and I glanced at each other and then pushed ourselves faster to get to him. Had he had a heart attack? He appeared to be in good physical condition, but looks could be deceiving.

When Alec and I got to him, we knelt at the same time, one on each side. Alec turned him over and felt for a pulse in his neck. He kept moving his fingers around, looking for the right spot.

"Alec," I gasped.

He looked at me, questioning.

I was out of breath and couldn't speak, so I pointed to a dark wet spot on his red running jacket.

"Oh," Alec said and unzipped the jacket. His shirt was white underneath his jacket, but it was turning bright crimson at an alarming pace. "I can't find a pulse," Alec said.

I swallowed, my heart pounding hard, but now it was from adrenaline.

"What happened?" I gasped.

Alec shook his head and kept feeling for a pulse.

I heard that same whistling noise I had heard before Todd fell, and the snow next to me puffed up into the air. Then it happened again and again. Each time, small puffs of snow and dirt flew up.

"Run!" Alec said, getting to his feet and grabbing my hand.

"What is it?" I screamed as I got to my feet, and we ran back in the direction we had come from.

"Someone's shooting at us," he said. "Do you have a phone on you?"

"No, it's in the car," I gasped.

"Run!" he repeated, pulling on my hand.

"Shooting?" I said, stunned. It seemed inconceivable.

He nodded. "Hurry."

I put on some speed and we headed back toward a small crowd of runners that had been behind us. I was too afraid to look behind me now. I didn't want to see someone running after us with a gun.

"Wait, Thad is in the other direction. We have to get to him!" I cried, coming to a sudden stop.

Alec grabbed my arm. "We have to get back to the Rec Center. We can't catch them," he said. "They'll get back to the Rec Center before we do if we chase after them."

I shook my head and pulled back, away from him. "No! That's my baby!"

"My gun is in my car. We are not running into the sights of a gunman. Thad and the other kids already passed the spot where Todd fell. They'll be back at the Rec Center within a few minutes," he said, breathing hard, and pulled me toward the group of runners coming toward us.

What he said made sense, but all I could think of was my kids. I wanted to see my kids. I wanted to see Thad right now.

"Go back!" Alec ordered the approaching runners. "Turn around!" he signaled to the runners with his hand, but they looked at him, confused, and kept running toward us. They didn't understand why he was telling them to go back.

"Turn around!" Alec gasped.

"What?" someone asked.

"What do you mean, turn around?" someone else asked.

"Someone's shooting at us!" I screamed.

That stopped them in their tracks.

"Get to shelter at the Rec Center!" Alec commanded.

Terror showed on their faces, and they turned to run back to the Rec Center building.

"What happened?" someone asked. "Who's shooting?"

"Run!" Alec ordered.

As we ran into more groups of runners and walkers, we ordered them back to the building. We had been ahead of almost everyone, except for Todd and the small group of five or six college-age runners, so we were able to get the rest headed back to the building before they got close to where Todd was hit.

"What about Thad and the other kids?" I gasped. It was hard for me to keep my wits about me. Would they really make it back to the Rec Center unharmed?

"They'll be okay, Allie. They were in the shooter's sights, and they weren't shot. They were moving at a fast pace. They'll be back at the Rec Center shortly."

I wanted to believe him, but I couldn't. Not until I actually saw Thad unharmed.

When we got to the door of the Rec Center, I looked over my shoulder, but there was no one there. The shooter hadn't followed us unless they were staying under cover of the trees.

"I have a gun in my car," he reminded me. "You get inside with everyone else." He gave me a push to get me inside, and he slammed the door behind me.

I stood by a window and watched him unlock the back of his SUV. He took out his gun holster and slung it on himself, and grabbed his phone. Then he headed back to the front door.

"Everyone on the floor!" he ordered when he saw people standing around. "Stay away from the windows and stay down on the floor." He made a call for backup, then stood near the window, watching.

Lucy hurried over and stood beside me.

"What's going on?" she asked, wide-eyed. "Why are we getting on the floor?"

"Get over here," I said, pulling her with me. We both dropped to the floor. "Todd Spellman was shot," I whispered. "And Thad is still out there!" My vision blurred as tears filled my eyes. I needed my son back, safe, and sound.

"What? Who shot him?" she whispered.

"I don't know. We didn't see anyone. I think they had a silencer on the gun," I whispered. I looked around to see if anyone was listening to our conversation.

"Oh my gosh. That's terrible," she whispered. "What about Thad? Where is he?"

"He and the other college kids were out ahead of everyone. They had already passed the spot where Todd was shot. Alec swears they'll be safe and be back here soon, but I just want my boy here now. What if something happens to him?" I asked. My voice cracked on the last part, and I wiped at my eyes with my gloved hand.

"It's okay," she said, grabbing my other hand and squeezing it. "He's a smart boy, and he's fast."

"What? What did you say?" Leann Riddle asked, inching toward us on the floor. Her long black hair had come out of its ponytail and fell across her face.

"Who got shot?" Leann asked, panic in her voice.

"Hush!" Lucy hissed. "You're going to panic people."

I hoped backup came quickly. Was there more than one shooter? My mind spun with thoughts of a mass shooting, and I tried to push them away.

"Are we going to be killed?" Luann Dobbs whimpered from her place on the floor near one of the windows.

My heart pounded. It was the question I was too afraid to ask.

"No, we are not going to be killed," Alec said, sounding confident. "Everyone needs to stay calm and stay on the floor. You're going to be fine." I hadn't heard his authoritative police voice before, and it turns out it was comforting. It made me want to believe him.

I looked around for Mr. Spellman. I hoped he didn't understand what was happening. I didn't want him to overhear anyone talking about what had happened to his son. He was sitting in his wheelchair near where I had last seen him. He was in a corner, away from the windows, and I thought he would be safe there.

"I want everyone to stay put. No one goes outside and stay away from the windows!" Alec ordered and went to the door. He opened it and looked around. I could feel a whoosh of cold air from where I lay on the floor.

"Alec, don't go back out there," I said. My heart jumped in my chest. I didn't want him out there with some murdering lunatic. "Wait for backup!"

He put a finger to his lips and slipped outside, closing the door behind himself.

Chapter Three

"OH, PLEASE," I SAID and fought back the tears that threatened to fall. I couldn't bear it if either Thad or Alec got hurt. I could hear soft crying from somewhere across the room, but I didn't look to see who it was. Everyone was scared, including me. I said a silent prayer for Thad and Alec's safety and hoped this nightmare would end soon.

Lucy put her hand on mine again. "It will be okay. Alec and Thad will be back soon."

I looked at her and nodded. She was right. Alec had been a police officer for years and had survived this long. He would be fine, I told myself. And Thad was fast. He would probably win the race without even knowing there was danger behind him.

"Did you see who was shot, Allie?" Ellen Allen inched her way over beside me and asked.

"I don't want to say," I said. I didn't want Mr. Spellman to hear about it this way. It looked like Todd was dead. If he wasn't, he soon would be if they didn't get an ambulance to him right away.

I could hear sirens in the distance, and I breathed a sigh of relief.

The door swung open, and we all jumped. I looked up, and Thad was the first one through the door, with the other college students behind him. I jumped up, forgetting about needing to stay on the floor, and ran to him and threw my arms around his neck.

"I'm so glad you're okay," I sobbed. "I was so scared."

"It's okay, Mom. I'm okay," he said, breathing hard. "Alec said to get on the floor."

We both got down on the floor, and I held his hand. My boy was safe.

The other college kids looked terrified and dropped to the floor near us. I was thankful they were all safe.

WE LAY ON THE FLOOR for what seemed like hours before Alec came back inside. In reality, it was probably less than an hour, but I had lost track of time. I just wanted this nightmare to be over.

"You're all free to get up off the floor now, but we want everyone to stay put for the time being," he announced. He pulled his phone out of his pocket and made a phone call, standing in the corner, away from everyone else.

"Why don't we have some pie?" I announced, getting to my feet. It would provide a distraction, and take our minds off of what had happened, at least for a few minutes.

"That's a good idea," Lucy said, jumping up and getting the Thanksgiving-themed paper plates and napkins together.

"Who wants pie?" I asked brightly, cutting into a pumpkin pie. I probably sounded like I was crazy, but I was trying for happy. The stress was getting to me.

People slowly got to their feet and began asking who was shot when the ambulance drove past the window.

"Why won't you tell us who got shot?" Ellen asked. She had a surly attitude after spending time on the hard floor, but then, she almost always had a surly attitude.

"Because it's police business. Would you want everyone standing around talking about it if it had been your mom that had gotten shot?" I asked. Some people could be so dense.

Ellen snorted. "My mom wouldn't be caught dead out there running in the snow."

I was going to point out the murder could have occurred anywhere, and thus her statement had no bearing but decided it wasn't going to make any difference, anyway. I cut a piece of pumpkin pie and slapped it onto a plate and handed it to her.

"I want apple pie," she protested, staring at the slice of pumpkin pie like it would poison her.

I gave her a hard look and cut her a piece of apple pie. Anything to get rid of her. That woman irritated me, even on a good day.

Ellen took her piece of pie, and I pasted a smile on my face. Here we all were, having pie and coffee and pretending a man had not just been murdered outside of this building. It was just like any other day, right? It wasn't like it was a major holiday, and someone wasn't going to be told their loved one was gone and wouldn't be home for dinner. I blew air out of my mouth and bit my lower lip to keep from crying.

I began cutting pieces of pie and handing them to Lucy and Thad to hand out. I didn't care who got what flavor, just as long as everyone had a piece to keep them occupied for a few minutes.

"May I have mincemeat?" Mr. Winters asked, standing in front of my table.

I looked at him and cocked an eyebrow. "Don't tell me you have information about the shooting already?" Mr. Winters was the town gossip and knew far more about what was going on in this town than anyone would think an elderly man would know. This was a fact that I had become aware of over the last couple of months, and his knowledge came in handy from time to time.

He gave me a big grin and flashed his partially gold canine tooth. "Nope. Not yet. But you can bet I soon will."

"It wouldn't surprise me a bit," I said, handing him a piece of mincemeat pie. I made a mental note to talk to Mr. Winters in a few days if the police hadn't come up with a suspect. It's called networking.

I couldn't imagine why someone would shoot Todd Spellman. He was the most personable individual I had ever met. He had a happy, upbeat personality and always took the time to talk to people. I mean, really talk to them. He looked you in the eye and gave you his full attention. I couldn't see how he could make any enemies.

But even scarier was the fact that they took shots at Alec and I. As far as I knew, I didn't have any enemies. Was this some crazed killer that would shoot at anyone? I had to wonder if Todd knew whether he had any enemies before he took a bullet to the chest. Did most people who were murdered know they had enemies before they died? Maybe this was just some rogue murderer that did it for sport. My mind was racing with thoughts, and I was going to have to run these ideas by Alec and see what he thought.

"Cherry, please," Eileen Smith said, stepping up for some pie.

"Coming right up," I said. "By the way, how badly is this delay going to hurt the community meal?"

We had raised money at the Halloween bazaar for the community Thanksgiving meal, as well as money to buy coats for underprivileged kids. The meal was being held at Henry's Home Cooking Restaurant, and Eileen Smith worked there.

"I hope not too much," she answered. "We made a lot of dishes in advance, and the turkeys were put in the oven to roast early this morning. The pies you brought are such a big help. If I can get out of here soon, we shouldn't have much of a delay."

"That's good to hear," I said. "I know there are people that depend on that meal every year."

"I know, so many people have mentioned they're going there," Lucy added. "I'm glad it's there for them."

I glanced over at Mr. Spellman, sitting by himself in the corner. I hoped he had family in town for the holiday that could take care of him. I handed Lucy the pie server and got a bottle of water and went over to Mr. Spellman.

"Are you thirsty, Mr. Spellman?" I asked. He didn't look at me, but when I put his hands around the bottle of water, he gripped it and held onto it.

He had been here for a couple of hours, and I wondered if he was hungry. I went and cut him a piece of my pecan pie and brought it to him. He looked at it and appeared interested, but his hands shook so much that I didn't think he could handle the fork. I didn't know whether he had issues feeding himself, but I decided to do it, just in case he was no longer capable of it.

Lucy came over to where we were and asked, "What do you think is happening out there?"

I shrugged and put a finger to my lips.

"Okay, sorry," she said. She looked at Mr. Spellman. "Are you enjoying that pecan pie, Mr. Spellman?"

He smiled and nodded.

"Can you help him?" I asked, handing her the plate. I wanted to talk to Alec.

He was still on the phone, so I went and stood by him and waited. When he finished, I asked, "Is he?"

He nodded. "I sent someone by the residence to see if anyone else was at home. Do you know if there's family nearby? I hate for Mr. Spellman to have to sit here much longer."

"I'm not sure. I think Todd had a sister, but I think she lived out of state. I had a conversation with him once at the health fair, and we talked about family. But I don't remember what state she was in. Hopefully she's in town for Thanksgiving. What sad news to have delivered on a holiday."

His mouth made a straight line. "It really is. It's sad news any day."

I nodded. "Did they find the shooter?" I asked.

He shook his head. "No, we're pretty sure they've left the area by now, but they'll continue to search for a while before sending everyone home. I'm afraid there are going to be some late Thanksgiving meals today."

"At least most of us will still be able to celebrate Thanksgiving," I said.

"That's true," he agreed.

"Can you release Eileen Smith so she can go back to Henry's to help fix the community Thanksgiving meal? It's kind of important. Even though there are others there working on it, it would be a big help to a lot of people to let her go."

"I don't see why not. I'll get Yancey to walk her to her car," he said. "I want you and Thad to go home with Lucy. I don't know what time I'll be by, but it will probably be much later."

"No, I want to stay with you," I insisted. After what had happened here today, I didn't want him out of my sight.

"No, you have your kids home, and you need to make the Thanksgiving meal for them. I'll be by as soon as I can," he said, slipping his phone into his pocket.

I sighed. He was right. I had a lot of work to do at home to get the meal prepared. "Promise me you'll be okay?" I asked.

"I promise," he said.

I looked at him, still not wanting to leave. I knew he was right. He would probably be here for hours. There really wasn't anything I could do here. "Okay. But call me if anything happens, okay?"

"Everything will be fine," he promised.

Chapter Four

IT WAS NEARLY 6:30 p.m., and Alec hadn't arrived for dinner yet. I had a houseful of hungry people and a turkey that was begging to be carved. I had looked out the living room window so many times I had worn a path to it from the kitchen.

"Mom, I'm starving. I'm going to McDonald's if we don't eat soon," Thad said, joining me in the kitchen. "I hate to do it to you, but that turkey is torturing me."

I turned around and looked at my son. He looked so much like his father, it hurt. And I only had him home for a few days. Along with his new girlfriend. A girlfriend I didn't know existed before they got on the plane.

"Give me ten minutes, and we'll eat. Here, have a Triscuit," I said, handing him the box. Triscuit crackers were Thanksgiving staples in my house when I was growing up in Alabama. You can't have Thanksgiving without them.

"Awesome," he said and took the box from me.

I raised him right.

I pulled the turkey out of the oven and set it on the counter to rest. My stomach growled, and I hoped I was going to be able to wait. We had escaped death today, and that was more than enough to work up an appetite. I hoped Alec would be able to get away soon. He had to be starving by now.

"What do you need help with?" Lucy asked. I had invited her and her husband Ed, my kids, plus Thad's new girlfriend, Sarah, and Alec. Only Alec was missing. He was still out looking for a killer.

"I think everything's about ready. We just need to get everything to the table," I said, wishing Alec was here.

"Don't worry, I'm sure he'll be here as soon as he can," she said, reading my mind.

"I know. I just wish it would be sooner rather than later," I answered. The doorbell rang, and I put down my potholder and hurried to the door.

"Hi," I said and tried not to cry when I opened the door and saw Alec on the step.

"Hi. Sorry I'm so late. I thought we'd be done before now," he said, sounding tired.

I held my arms out, and he stepped forward, allowing me to hold him tight before he came inside, and I would have to share him with everyone else. "It's understandable," I said and led him into the living room.

I introduced Alec to everyone he didn't already know and immediately got the stink eye from my daughter Jennifer. I ignored her. She would just have to learn to deal with the fact that Alec wasn't going away. At least, not if I could help it.

"Why don't we all head to the dinner table?" I suggested. "You must be starving, Alec."

"Well, the truth is, I am," he said with a grin.

"Oh, here, have a Triscuit," Thad said, holding the box out.

Alec looked at me, questioning. I shook my head. "Pay no attention."

Lucy and I got dinner on the table within two minutes. It was a beautiful sight. I had made the turkey, yams, cranberry sauce, stuffing, five different pies, and a pear cranberry tart that screamed Thanksgiving. Lucy had made a cheesy broccoli casserole and a green bean casserole. Jennifer contributed a potato salad and buttermilk biscuits that would melt in your mouth. Sarah made, well, she made something that resembled an orange gelatin salad. But I wasn't complaining. Everything was perfect.

And then suddenly, I had a dilemma. Ever since my husband had passed away, Thad had taken over turkey carving duties. But Alec was my boyfriend, albeit a new one. Should he do it? I glanced over at him. In my Southern family, it was tradition for the husband or significant other of the woman of the house to do it. Or a grandfather. Old fashioned, to be sure, but I didn't know any other way. Then Thad picked up the knife, and I shook my head. I was being silly. Thad should be the one to do it. I hadn't been dating Alec long enough to think otherwise.

Thad was an excellent turkey carver, and he handled the task with ease. It made me proud to watch him. I glanced over at Sarah. I could see she was proud, too. Her eyes shone as she gazed at him. There was a part of me that bristled at the way she looked at him. Maybe it was the same for Jennifer when she looked at Alec and me. I reminded myself to be nice.

"So was the shooter caught? How is the investigation going?" I asked as we passed serving bowls around.

"It's going as well as can be expected," Alec said. "Still no suspect in custody, and it's too dark outside to do anything further tonight."

"What happened with Mr. Spellman?" I asked.

"That poor man," Lucy added.

"His daughter and her husband were indeed visiting. I don't think he understood what was going on, and his daughter was going to talk with him after I left."

"That's wild," Thad said. "Someone just shot his son dead during the Turkey Trot."

Alec nodded. "It's terrible."

"Hopefully the murderer will be caught soon," I said, serving myself some cranberry sauce.

"Well, maybe it was just a hunter that accidentally shot him?" Jennifer suggested with more than a little attitude. "I mean, what if everyone's jumping to conclusions? How does anyone know it was a murder?"

"It's highly unlikely," Alec said. "It looks very calculated from the preliminary investigation. That could change as we get further into it, of course."

"Yeah, but you don't know. What if it was some kid trying to get his first deer and the poor kid made a mistake and hit that guy? How terrible do you think he's going to feel, not only at having killed someone but now everyone thinks he's a murderer and they're passing that around town like it's the truth?"

All eyes were on Jennifer. She was getting far too invested in some little kid that may not even exist.

"Well, that hardly seems plausible. The Turkey Trot was highly advertised, and there was a fairly large group out running or walking in the area," Alec explained patiently. "I don't think anyone would make the mistake of hunting that close to the Rec Center."

"You don't know. You don't know anything yet," she said, sulking. She stabbed a green bean with her fork.

"If it was a kid, don't you think he would have stuck around to explain himself?" Thad pointed out.

"Not if he's scared! He might have run off when he realized what he did." Her cheeks turned pink.

"Jennifer, I think if it was some kid trying to shoot a deer, then he wouldn't have shot at Alec and me after hitting Todd," I said, giving her my best 'mama's about to get mad' look.

Jennifer narrowed her eyes at me and stuck a piece of turkey in her mouth. I tried not to sigh too loudly. The girl needed to calm down. I glanced at Alec and gave him an apologetic smile.

He grinned and cut into his candied sweet potatoes with the edge of his fork. "These are awesome," he said after taking a bite.

"Thanks. That's my mama's recipe."

Sarah was still staring at Thad, and it was starting to bug me. "Sarah, would you like some gravy?" I asked. She was a girl of few words, and I was beginning to wonder if she ever talked.

She turned to me and smiled. "Yes, thank you."

I handed over the gravy boat and smiled back at her. I wanted a real conversation with the girl. "So tell me, Sarah, what are you studying at school?"

"Comic Art," Sarah said.

I looked at her, confused. "What? What's that?"

"It's the study of comics as art. It's also about teaching technique," she said and poured gravy over her turkey.

"Comics? Like in the Sunday paper?" I asked, puzzled.

"Yes. But there are other sources of comics these days."

I stared at her and then looked at Thad. He had a tiny smirk on his face. "Is she serious?" I asked him. Surely she had to be teasing me.

He nodded. "Comics have become very big since the advent of the Internet, Mom. Actually, they've been big since the advent of, well, comics. You should check it out. You know, the Internet? A newspaper, maybe?"

I gave him the stink eye. "I've been to the Internet. I'm well acquainted with it, considering I write a blog. I've even read a newspaper or two."

"Comic art is very important to our generation, Mrs. McSwain," Sarah explained. "We've lived all our lives surrounded by them, from comic books, to the Sunday comic pages, to artwork, to video games. Our society would not have evolved like it has if there were no comics."

I stared at her. Before now, I hadn't thought she knew that many words. And I was pretty sure society would have evolved just fine without comics. It took all I had to keep from making a smart remark. "Really?" was all I could come up with that wouldn't have been offensive at that point.

She nodded very seriously. "Just look at the advent and rise of Comic-Con and all the resultant 'cons.' It's an important art form."

"I like Archie comics, myself," Lucy said, buttering a biscuit.

"Comics are nice," Alec added noncommittally.

I glanced at Alec and then at Lucy and Ed. Ed had so far remained silent, and I thought he might be the smartest man in the room.

"I see," I finally said to Sarah.

"Mom, you need to expand your horizons," Thad said, leaning back in his chair and putting one arm across the back of Sarah's chair.

"I've heard of Comic-Con," Ed finally said, digging into a pile of mashed potatoes. "I'd like to go to one."

"What kind of job are you looking at when you graduate, Sarah? Are you a junior, like Thad?" I asked her, ignoring the others.

"Well," she said, pushing her glasses further up on her nose. She had blond hair with a streak of red dyed hair on one side and a smattering of freckles on her nose. She was a cute girl, but she had me worried with this comic business. "I'm thinking about adding Internet studies to my major. I want to create websites for the Post-Millennial generation. And yes, I'm a junior just like Thad."

I looked at Thad. Thad was majoring in criminal law. What was he doing with this girl? Maybe I was letting my age show, but it seemed highly improbable that she was going to make a living creating websites and comics for the Internet. She seemed intelligent, except for her decision on her college major, so maybe I was underestimating her. But I had my doubts about her career choice after college.

"And what do your parents think of your college major?" I asked.

"They're all for it," she said with a smile.

I nodded. Of course they were.

I turned to Alec. "Are you going to be tied up with the investigation tomorrow?"

"I'm going to let the officers finish investigating the crime scene. I've been over it pretty thoroughly myself, but sometimes another pair or two of eyes will discover something I didn't," he answered. "I'll probably go over it again later, after they do their part, though. I'm kind of OCD that way."

I smiled. "Good. Let's go Black Friday shopping first thing in the morning."

He chuckled. "I haven't done that in years, and as I recall, I never did enjoy it."

"Good, it's settled then," I said, grinning at him. Shopping was therapy for me, and after the day I had had, I needed some therapy. Plus, the sales were always good on Black Friday.

Chapter Five

"HEY!" I CRIED OUT AS a teenage boy ran past me, hip-checking me as he went.

I heard Alec chuckle. "Well, you did want to go Black Friday shopping."

I gave him a look, narrowing my eyes at him. "You get the best deals today. It's worth a few bruises. But next time, can you trip whoever runs into me so they'll at least get some bruises, too?"

"Oh, sure. No problem," he said, leaning against the display of shoes. We were at Kohl's, and it was just after 5:00 a.m. Most of the athletic shoes were forty percent off, and I was going to get ten dollars in Kohl's cash for every fifty dollars I spent. Believe me, it was worth the hassle of the crowds to get running shoes that cheap. I planned on stocking up on them.

"You need to try some of these on. I'm sure you wear them out just as fast as I do."

"Where would you propose I try them on?" he asked, looking around at the crowded shoe department.

He was right. The display was being swarmed by every runner and non-runner in the county. The benches to try shoes on were filled with bleary-eyed shoppers, many with kids in tow, and open boxes and stray shoes lay all over the place.

I grabbed a cute pair of neon green and orange ones and sat on the floor next to where he stood to try them on. "See? It's not so hard," I said, looking up at him.

He smirked. "Okay, let's see," he said, grabbing a pair of Nike in classic black with a white swoosh in a size twelve. He sat on the floor next to me and took his shoe off.

I stood up to get a feel of the new shoes I was trying on. They were a little tight, but the aisles were stuffed with people, and I wasn't sure I could get a look to see if I could find the same style in a half size larger. Instead, I grabbed a pair of electric blue with a yellow swoosh and sat back down.

"Those are stylish," he said, looking at mine. "Maybe I should look for hot pink in my size?" He stood up and took a few steps to try to get a feel for the pair he had on.

"Good luck with that," I said, slipping the new shoe on. It felt good. "I am determined to get at least three pairs of running shoes today."

"I guess I should get a couple, too," he said and scooted as close to the shelves as he dared. He reached over a teenaged boy to grab a box of shoes, only to have the kid turn and give him the evil eye.

"That's mine," the kid protested. He was on the small side and wasn't much over five feet tall.

Alec looked at his feet. "Nice try, but maybe you can fill these shoes in another ten years," he said and came back to where I sat.

"Ouch," I said as he grinned at me.

Before he could sit down, Bob Payne came around the corner and nearly collided with him.

"Hey, look out!" Bob said, and then his eyes got big when he realized who it was that he had nearly run down.

"Excuse me?" Alec said, just as surprised to see Bob as Bob was to see him.

Bob frowned and huffed air out of his mouth.

"Excuse me," he said, and tried to go around Alec, but an elderly woman with a walker blocked his path.

Bob Payne was the part-time mayor of Sandy Harbor. "So, Bob, I'm sorry to hear about Todd Spellman. I'm sure he'll be missed," I said. Todd Spellman had been Bob's boss at the Bank of Maine. I figured since he was here, I may as well see if he had anything to say about what had happened the previous day. He had not been in attendance at the Turkey Trot since it wasn't being held on a golf course, and golf was all he seemed to be interested in, but I figured he knew plenty about what happened by now.

"Oh? Are you? Because I'm sorry my mother had to spend Thanksgiving in jail, seeing as how the judge denied bail. Flight risk! She's sixty-six years old!" he said, looking at me.

Bob's mother had recently been arrested, and it sounded like she wasn't enjoying jail very much.

"Oh, I'm sorry. But since you have relatives in Canada, it is conceivable that she might take a little trip. You know, for the holidays?" I pointed out. "I mean, she did confess to a crime, and she also tried to kill Alec and me."

Bob rolled his eyes at me. "She was a little tipsy. She didn't know what she was saying. And there weren't any bullets in the gun she threatened you with," he said, putting his hands on his hips.

"When a gun's pointing at you, you have to assume it has bullets," Alec pointed out. "It's a good thing I didn't go for my gun, or your mother would have spent Thanksgiving in a completely different place."

Bob looked at Alec and made a face. "Do you know that I had to take my two daughters down to that filthy place to visit with their grandmother for Thanksgiving? We had to tell them Grandma was at a spa and couldn't come home. I was mortified when they searched all of us. They searched my six-year-old," he hissed.

I pressed my lips together to keep from laughing. And then I snickered. I couldn't help it. Bob lived in another world if he thought he could tell his daughters that the county lockup was a spa and they would believe it.

He gasped. "How dare you."

"Okay, I'm sorry your little girls had to go through that. I really am. But eventually you are going to have to tell them the truth."

"It's none of your business," he hissed, and tried to get around the little old lady, but she had stopped what she was doing to listen to our conversation and was effectively blocking Bob's intended departure route.

"Bob, is there any chance you know anything about what happened with Todd?" Alec asked.

Bob was doing a little side-to-side dance with the little elderly lady mirroring his movements. He made a sound in his throat and then turned back to Alec. "I have no idea. But I'll tell you one thing. There will be more people glad he's gone than sorry about it."

"Really?" Alec asked, eyebrows raised.

"I don't believe it. Todd was an outstanding member of the community," I said, hoping he would spill the beans on the situation.

"I don't care what you believe, Allie McSwain. That Todd was a nightmare to work for."

"Really? Because I think he was a saint. A saint slain in the prime of his life. What will Sandy Harbor do without him? He was a leader in this town. We've lost two leaders in two months. I, for one, am outraged." I was laying it on thick in hopes of getting him to talk.

Bob's face turned two shades of red. "Todd was a nasty, hostile jerk. Oh sure, he put on another face for everyone around town to see, but those of us that worked for him knew better. He was rude and callous, and... and rude."

I tried not to look at Alec. I knew he was taking this all in, and I half-expected to see him whip out his trusty pen and notebook any minute.

"That's interesting. Because I heard he was the biggest giver at the Halloween bazaar. He loved those unfortunate children from the poor side of town and wanted them all to have nice winter coats," I said, standing up and trying to get a feel for the new pair of shoes.

Bob sighed loudly as the little elderly lady decided to move on, slowly picking up her walker and placing it four inches out in front of her, and then shuffling two steps forward.

"Look, you can believe what you want. But his last words to us when we left work on Wednesday were, I hope the riff-raff from the south side of town don't show up for free pie at the Turkey Trot because I can hardly stand the smell of them."

I stared at him. I had to admit that that *was* rude.

"Everyone at work hated him," he said quietly.

"Everyone?" I asked.

He nodded his head furiously.

"It sounds like you had some real issues with Todd," Alec said.

Bob's balding head whipped around to look at Alec. "What? No, I didn't. I mean, sure, he was a pain, but what boss isn't? Look, I may not have cared much for the way he did things, but I did not have a beef with him."

"Do you know who might have?" Alec asked.

Bob shook his head. "No. I don't have any idea. Look, I don't want any trouble. I just need to pick up some shoes for my kids. I don't know anything about this murder."

"Don't get excited, Bob. I'm just asking a question. If you can think of anything later, I'm sure you'll let me know, right?" Alec said, very calm and matter-of-factly.

"Of course I will," he agreed. "I'm going to get going now."

"See you around," I said to his back as he made a hasty exit.

Alec sat on the floor to try on another pair of shoes he had picked up, and I sat next to him.

"What do you make of that?" I whispered.

"I'm not sure just yet," he said, lacing up the red and white shoe. "I'll have to keep my eyes and ears open and see where it leads."

"I say we go down and interview everyone at the bank. See if their stories line up with Bob's."

Alec cleared his throat and put the other shoe on. "You mean *I. I'll* look into their stories."

"Okay, but you know every ace detective needs a sidekick, and I'm your woman."

Alec snorted. "I haven't needed one before now."

"You know, yesterday when I took Mr. Spellman a cup of coffee, I had a little conversation with him. Not that he had much to say, mind you. But it seemed like there was something there. Like he was trying to tell me something with his eyes, and whatever it was, it scared him," I said, ignoring his comment.

"Yeah?" he asked.

"Yeah. I like the red. It's very sexy," I said, looking at his shoes.

"And when you're running down the trail, sweating and stinking, sexy is important," he said.

"You're darned right," I assured him.

He got up and went to look for another pair of shoes.

*Todd wasn't what he seem*ed, I thought.

Chapter Six

IT WAS LATE AFTERNOON on Black Friday, and I had shopped until I nearly dropped, and then shopped some more. Alec had left me off at home an hour earlier. I should have stayed home in front of the warm fire, but I was on the go again, and the cold air was making my cheeks hurt. I pulled my scarf up to cover the lower half of my face and watched the ground carefully as I walked. The snow had melted, but the ground was good and frozen. I held two cups of coffee in a cardboard drink carrier and scanned the area for Alec.

I could see something moving in the nearby thicket, and I stopped. Was that a deer? I took another step forward, and a dry twig snapped under my foot. There was a flash from behind the thicket, and Alec jumped out from behind it with his gun drawn. I screamed.

"Allie!" he shouted. "What are you doing here?"

I stopped screaming at him and tried to catch my breath. "I brought you coffee," I said weakly, holding up the drink carrier and smiling behind my scarf. My nose was running, and I sniffed.

"Seriously, Allie? You could have gotten yourself killed." Alec was frowning at me, and I could see the hard set of his eyes.

"I'm sorry," I said and held the drink carrier out to him again.

"Why are you sneaking up behind me like that?" he asked, moving toward me.

"I didn't want to startle you."

He rolled his eyes. "Well, that worked out just fine."

"Sorry," I repeated. I had thought I could assist him, but I didn't want to ask him first if it was okay. He always seemed to resist my assistance for some reason, even though I thought I was a pretty big help to him.

He blew air out through his mouth. "Come on, Allie, you shouldn't be out here. Do you know how I would have felt if I had shot you?"

"You're right. I shouldn't have come. But now I'm here and I brought coffee," I said brightly. The man just needed to focus on the fact that I had brought him coffee and he would lighten up, I was sure of it.

"Thanks," he said reluctantly and took a cup from me. He wore a long trench coat that I thought only television detectives wore. He had black boots on and earmuffs and looked like a city slicker taking his first jaunt into the woods. I tried to suppress a smile.

"I have cream and sugar," I said, pulling out packets from my coat pocket.

He took some of them and poured both cream and sugar into his coffee. "Thanks again." He sounded a little reluctant to say it, but he was warming up to my gift of coffee.

"You're welcome," I said. "So have you found out anything new about the case?"

"There's not a lot to go on. I found some spent casings, but not much else. They climbed up into this deer stand to shoot from," he said, motioning toward a deer stand. It was odd. I hadn't noticed one being here before.

"Well, maybe if I help you, we can find something new," I said, setting the drink carrier on the ground. I walked over to the deer stand and stood beneath it. We were deeper into the woods than where we had been when Todd was shot, but it wasn't that deep. "Isn't it weird that there's a deer stand this close to the Rec Center? I mean, sure, it's in the woods, but you would have to expect people to be in the area at any time. It's not a good place to be shooting a gun."

"Yeah, it's odd all right. The lumber used is old, but if you take a look, the nails used on it are clean. No rust. They haven't been out here in the weather long."

The stand was very rudimentary with a platform and a crude makeshift ladder attached. Some deer stands were fancier than this. I'd seen some that were fully enclosed with walls and a roof, and a separate platform to stand on.

"I'm not a hunter, but I wouldn't want to have to spend a lot of time on this thing in inclement weather," I said.

"Exactly. It appears to be very temporary and crudely put together."

"But if you knew when your deer was going to come by, say, at a scheduled time, you would only have to spend so much time on it," I surmised.

"Come on, let me show you something," he said. He went over to the deer stand, put his coffee cup on the ground, and climbed up to the platform. He looked down at me. "Come on."

"Me? That doesn't look safe," I said, shaking my head.

"You wanted to play detective," he said. "Come on up."

I moved over to the ladder and put my coffee on the ground, careful to find a stable place for it. Coffee was precious, and I didn't want to spill it.

I put my gloved hands on the crude ladder and pulled myself up to the first rung. The stand shuddered with my weight. I looked up at Alec. "Is it going to hold both of us?"

"It should. Come on up," he said, squatting down on the platform.

"Should? Sure doesn't make me feel warm and fuzzy," I said and moved up to the next rung. The ladder shuddered again, and I closed my eyes and pulled myself up the rest of the way. Climbing this thing was like pulling off a Band-Aid. Better to do it all at once.

"See now, that's not so bad, is it?" he teased as I made it to the platform.

"Well, it kind of is," I said, pulling myself up onto the platform. The stand shuddered again. I couldn't tell for sure, but I thought it listed to the side a little.

"Look," he said, pointing out to the woods.

"Oh, wow," I said. We had the perfect view of what looked like the exact spot that Todd Spellman had fallen. There was an opening in the trees that didn't look natural.

"Yeah. Todd had an enemy."

"If Bob is to be believed, it could be any one of his employees," I said. A breeze stirred, and the deer stand creaked. "Okay, time to get down." I moved the couple of steps back to the ladder and started down.

Alec chuckled. "Don't be a 'fraidy cat," he said.

"I will be a 'fraidy cat if I want to," I said. Feeling my feet hit solid ground, I let my breath out. I picked up my coffee and watched him climb down.

"Come on," he said and led the way through the woods.

"What kind of gun do you think it was?" I asked.

"We won't know exactly until we get the bullet from Todd Spellman's body examined by forensics, but it was a long gun of some type. Fitted with a silencer which is why we didn't hear it," he said as we walked.

"I heard a whistling noise. It's creepy, knowing what it was now. I thought silencers were against the law?" I asked.

"Only in some states. Not Maine. They do have to fill out extra paperwork at the time of purchase, but honestly, it wouldn't surprise me if it was stolen."

We walked a ways into the woods.

"Is this—" I asked when he stopped.

"Yes, this is where he was shot. See the trees? The killer cut off some branches, so they had a clear view," he said, pointing to the nearby trees.

I looked at the ground and was relieved I didn't see blood. "I would hate to know what they would have done if he had been in a pack of runners at the time he passed this spot," I said, shuddering.

"Since they didn't hesitate to fire at us, I think we both know what they would have done," he said. "The deer stand is due to be dismantled later today and brought to the lab in Bangor. It was already dusted for prints, but there wasn't anything. Maybe the lab will have better luck finding something."

"Do you think the killer might have come back to the area and tampered with anything?" I asked. I had walked past the crime scene tape.

"George spent last night in his squad car right out here in the middle of things. I don't think they could have. Just about everything has been removed and photographed at this point, except for the stand. I just wanted to go over things again, to be sure nothing was overlooked. I would have caught you entering the area had I been expecting you to be so nosy. Of course, I don't know why I didn't expect you to be."

I smiled at him. "You know me."

"That I do. As soon as Yancey and George return to get the deer stand, I'll go back to the office. Tomorrow morning I'm going to have a chat with Todd's family. They were initially questioned by Sam Bailey, but he didn't seem to think there was much there. Just a grieving family," he said.

"How did Mr. Spellman take it?" I asked.

He shrugged. "Sam seems to think he might have been given a sedative of some sort. Probably due to the stress of it all. He was really out of it. Maybe he'll be more alert when I go over there."

"Take me with you?" I asked hopefully.

He sighed. "Well, if I don't, what are the chances you'll sneak up on me from behind while I'm there?"

"Pretty good," I said, nodding.

"I figured as much."

Chapter Seven

"YOU KNOW THE DRILL, right?" Alec asked as he turned down Taylor Street.

"Yes, keep my mouth shut and just observe," I answered. The window of his SUV kept fogging up from the cold, even with the defroster running full blast. I leaned forward and wiped my sleeve over the front of the windshield so I could see.

"You know I'm on to you, right?" he asked.

"What do you mean?" I asked, turning toward him.

"'Keep your mouth shut and observe' is your code for 'ask a lot of questions and make accusations.' I'm catching on to you," he said with a small smile on his lips.

I grinned. "I don't know what you're talking about," I said, turning to look forward. The City was hanging Christmas lights. There would be a Christmas parade on the first of December, always at night, under the Christmas lights. An old familiar ache tugged at my heart. My kids had lived for that parade when they were small, and no matter how cold it was, my husband Thaddeus bundled them up, and we went to watch all the homemade floats, marching bands, and horse riders. There was nothing like Christmas in a small town.

"All right, plead the fifth if you must. But I'm not buying it."

I chuckled. He hadn't put up much of a fight when I told him I wanted to go with him to speak to Todd's family, and I was glad of that. I hated it when I had to beg.

He pulled up to the Spellman's house, and I could see a light on inside. It was just after eight, and I had wondered if anyone would be up and about yet.

We got out of the car and headed to the front door.

A tall woman with graying hair and bifocal glasses opened the door and peered at us for a moment before speaking. I could smell coffee brewing from inside the open door. "Yes?" she said. I guessed she must be close to sixty.

"Good morning, ma'am, I'm detective Alec Blanchard, and this is Allie McSwain. May we have a few minutes of your time?"

She took a step back and hesitated, then looked over her shoulder. Her face was free of wrinkles, and I decided my first guess was wrong. She was younger than sixty. The gray hair and bifocals aged her, but in a better light, she looked to be in her mid to late forties.

She turned back to us. "Yes, of course," she said and held the door open. "We're just getting up and around. I'm Connie Sutter, Todd's sister."

"Thank you," Alec said, and we followed her as she headed down the hall.

She led us into a formal living room that looked like it had been decorated in the early nineties and had not been sat in since.

"Let me get my husband. Would you like coffee?" she asked over her shoulder as she headed out the door we had come through.

"Yes, please," I said before Alec could answer. Coffee would allow us a few extra minutes of time here. I was curious about the life of Todd Spellman. He was the kind of person that nearly everyone in town knew because of his philanthropic endeavors. But after what Bob had said, if it was true, made me wonder if anyone really knew him at all.

A balding middle-aged man entered the room. He stopped, straightened his glasses, and gave us a pinched smile. "Hello, I'm Terrence Sutter, Todd's brother-in-law," he said, extending a hand to Alec and then to me.

Alec introduced us. "I'm sorry for your loss. We understand it's a difficult time for your whole family, but we have a few questions."

"Yes, of course," he said, and came over to sit on the sofa across from us. "We've been expecting you."

"How is Mr. Spellman?" I asked. I knew he had to be devastated over the loss of his son.

"Dad's doing as well as can be expected. The doctor gave him something to settle his nerves. He already had some minor sleep issues before this happened, and he needed a little help after being told the news."

"Of course," I said. I didn't blame Mr. Spellman one bit. I had needed to rely on medication for a month or longer after my husband had died.

"Mr. Sutter, do you know if there was anyone in your brother-in-law's life that wanted to harm him?" Alec asked.

"Please, call me Terrence. And no, I had never heard him say he had any issues with anyone," Terrence said with a shrug. He put on a smile and glanced at the living room door.

"Did he ever discuss his job?" Alec asked.

Terrence shook his head. "No, never. This is all so devastating, you know."

"I can imagine," Alec said sympathetically. "Any death is difficult, and murder makes it more so."

Connie Sutter entered the room holding a silver tray with four cups of coffee and a creamer and sugar bowl. She set the tray down on the coffee table with a carafe of coffee. "Please, help yourselves," she said, motioning toward the tray and giving us a strained smile. She sat next to her husband. My heart went out to her. How terrible to lose a loved one during the holidays.

"I'll ask you the same things I asked your husband, Mrs. Sutter. Did Todd ever mention having any trouble with anyone, or perhaps problems at work?" Alec asked, reaching for a cup of coffee and a spoon.

"No, he never discussed work, and he never had a bad thing to say about anyone," Mrs. Sutter said. "He was always so thoughtful of others." Her voice cracked, and she looked away.

"I'm sorry, Mrs. Sutter," Alec said. "I only have a few more questions, and then we'll leave you alone."

I looked at the silver tray and reached for a cup, running my finger over the tray. It was plastic beneath a silver coating. I looked around the room. The walls were filled with paintings in gold-trimmed frames. I poured myself a cup of coffee and added cream and sugar, and then I got up while Alec asked his questions and wandered over to a beautiful landscape painting.

There were snow-covered mountaintops with an impossibly blue sky, two paintings with river scenes, and several more with ponds.

The mountain painting reminded me of something you only saw in a foreign country. Perhaps Sweden or Switzerland. I took a closer look. At first glance, everything seemed expensive, but upon further inspection, a different story was revealed. The frames were plastic, and in places, the gold paint was flaking off. The painting itself was under glass, and I wondered if it was actually a print.

It reminded me of a television show set. I wondered if Todd had merely been thrifty or if he had wanted to keep up appearances by making others think he had invested a lot of money in the paintings. Maybe all his charity work was to cover up for something he lacked. Or felt that he lacked.

"That's an original painting by a famous artist. The Swiss Alps," Mrs. Sutter said, coming up behind me.

I jumped a little. I hadn't heard her get up. "Oh, it's lovely," I said.

"Yes, Todd was quite the art aficionado," she said, smiling at the painting.

I looked at her curiously. It didn't take much to see that the painting was a cheap knock off, and it wasn't just because the frames were inexpensive. The paintings were under glass, and authentic paintings usually weren't displayed like that.

"Todd was so involved in the community," I said. "He will be missed."

The smile left her lips. "Yes, he certainly will. He'll be missed by many people."

"I'm sorry for your loss, Mrs. Sutter," I said. I decided she must just be clueless about art.

She sniffed. "Please, call me Connie."

"Connie, where do you and your husband live?" I asked.

"Michigan. I wish we had taken the time to come to visit more often, but you know how it is. Life gets in the way, and you always think you have time. Until there is no more time," she said, her voice cracking on the last part.

"That's the truth," I said. "Will you be taking Mr. Spellman back to Michigan with you?"

"Oh, of course. Daddy is going to have such a hard time with this. We want to do all we can to help him through it."

"I would imagine having him close will also help you through your grief. I write a blog on grief. I've written a lot of articles on working through the process. It's called 'Working Through Grief'," I said. "I'll get you a business card with the web address on it if you want to take a look at it."

"That's very thoughtful of you," she said. "Yes, family is everything, and I know having my father home with me will be a help to both of us."

"Can we see Mr. Spellman before we leave? So we can pay our respects?" I asked.

"Oh, I'm sorry, but he's still sleeping. He's had such a hard time getting to sleep, and the meds the doctor gave him make it a little hard for him to wake up," she said, repeating what her husband had said.

"Oh, of course," I said, feeling a little disappointed. I had really wanted to check in on him.

Alec finished up with his questions, and I gave Connie my business card before we left.

"Well, how did that go?" I asked him as he pulled away from the curb.

He shrugged. "I didn't discover anything new or unusual. With them living so far away, it would be hard for them to know many details of Todd's life."

I nodded, thinking about the fake paintings. I couldn't imagine how anyone could be fooled by them, but perhaps Connie and her husband were just unfamiliar with artwork.

Chapter Eight

SUNDAY CAME FAR TOO soon, and it was time to say goodbye to Thad. Five days just weren't enough.

"Do you have everything packed?" I asked, hovering near him. His suitcase was still open on the bed.

"I think I do," he said, rummaging through his toiletry case.

"You know, Thad, you could easily transfer to the University of Maine to finish your studies. It would be so nice to have you closer," I said. I had tried not to meddle and coerce him into moving home, but I couldn't help it. The few weeks a year that I got to see him just weren't enough.

He smiled without looking at me. "I know, Mom. I wish Wisconsin wasn't so far away, too."

I sighed and swallowed the lump in my throat. "I know, you're all grown up, and you don't need me anymore." I couldn't help the dramatics. I was feeling sorry for myself.

"Now, Mom, you know that isn't true," he said. He turned toward me and had me in a bear hug before I knew what happened. I let loose with the tears then. There wasn't anything I could do to stop them. "Don't do that, Mom," he said softly.

"I know, I'm sorry," I whispered.

"So what's going on in here?" Sarah asked brightly, suddenly appearing in the doorway.

I pulled away and wiped my eyes with the back of my hand. "Nothing," I said and left the room, heading for the living room. I needed to pull myself together. He was all grown up now, and he had a life to live. That's what his father and I had raised him to do.

"What's going on?" Jennifer asked, sliding her slipper clad feet across the hardwood floors in the living room.

"Oh, nothing. Your brother's getting ready to leave," I said, and went to the kitchen to pour myself a cup of coffee. I needed a good strong shot of caffeine to perk up my mood.

"I can drive him to the airport if you want," she said, taking a mug from the cupboard.

I thought to protest because I wanted the last few minutes with Thad, but then I thought better of it. I could cry here in private, instead of at the airport where all the holiday travelers were milling about. I didn't need an audience.

"That sounds good. But you better get dressed or he'll be late for his plane. They, I mean. They'll be late for their plane," I corrected myself. I couldn't forget Sarah, although I wanted to. I needed to get over this and fast. Thad seemed to be serious about Sarah, and I needed to make her feel welcome, in case this became a permanent thing. I shuddered at the thought.

"Got it," she said, pouring herself a cup of coffee. "It won't take but a few minutes for me to be ready."

I poured myself some coffee and went and sat on the sofa. I picked up the Bangor morning paper and read the headlines.

MAN SHOT DEAD DURING ANNUAL SANDY HARBOR TURKEY TROT

The article beneath it rehashed what I already knew. There wasn't anything new to be told, and if there was, I was pretty sure Alec would have let me know about it. I sighed and wondered where the murderer was this morning. Probably gloating that they had gotten away with it.

"Okay, I guess we're ready," Thad announced, carrying out his and Sarah's suitcases. He was bundled up in a jacket and wore a black knit hat.

I smiled at him. "I still can't get over how much you look like your dad."

He gave me a big smile. "But I have your winning personality."

I laughed and went to give him a final hug. "That, you do." My eyes teared up again, and Sarah came up from behind him. I didn't care. I had almost lost my only son a few days earlier, and I was going to cry. "I'm so glad you're safe."

"I know, Mom, I am too. I'm even more glad that you're safe," he said, squeezing me tight.

"All right, enough with the familial love fest. We gotta get a move on," Jennifer said, entering the room, now fully dressed and with proper shoes on her feet.

I sighed, pushed away, and held Thad at arm's length. "Call me when you get back to Wisconsin."

He nodded. "You know I will."

I said my goodbyes to Sarah, and in a moment, they were gone. I watched through the living room window until Jennifer's car was out of sight. The phone in the kitchen rang, and I hurried to get it before the caller hung up.

I grabbed the receiver on the third ring and had just a moment to glance at Caller ID. *Todd Spellman*. My heart leaped in my chest.

"Hello?" I said.

There was silence on the other end.

"Hello?" I repeated. There was still no answer, and I glanced at the Caller ID again. *Todd Spellman*. "Hello? Who is this?" There was only silence on the other end of the line. "Hello?" There was a bit of static, then silence again. "Hello?"

I waited for what seemed like forever before hanging up and watched the name Todd Spellman disappear from the display. I took three steps back, still staring at the phone. *What was that all about*?

The hair on the back of my neck stood up as I remembered the last phone call I had gotten on this phone. It was last month and was from a soon-to-be-deceased Diana Bowen. Of course, she didn't know she was about to be deceased when she made the phone call, but still. By the time I had listened to the voicemail, Diana was already dead, and it was creepy. And this was creepy too since I had never called Todd while he was alive. And I certainly wasn't going to call him now that he was dead.

I took another step back. That phone needed to be removed. Having dead people call me put a damper on the day. I went in search of my cell phone. I had wanted to call Alec anyway, and now I needed to hear the voice of a real, live person.

I found my phone on my nightstand and saw that I had missed a call from Alec. I hit redial and let my breath out when he answered.

"Alec, I just got a call from Todd Spellman on my house phone, and there wasn't anyone on the other end of the line!" I spat out before he could say anything more than hello.

"Really?" he said. "I didn't know there was a phone down at the morgue for him to use."

"Really?" I almost exploded. "That's all you have to say about it?"

"Whoa, hold on, Allie. I'm sorry. I was only teasing. Maybe one of the Spellman's wanted to speak to you since you accompanied me to talk to them yesterday. I didn't mean to make fun of you, I promise."

I took a deep breath. I may have been overreacting. "Okay, sorry. I shouldn't have gotten so upset. It's weird though. Don't you think?"

"It is. Maybe we'll pay them another visit soon," he said.

"Why wouldn't they speak when I said hello over and over?" I asked, trying to keep the whine out of my voice.

"Maybe it was a bad connection? No one uses house phones much anymore. Maybe with the snow, it was just a bad connection?" he suggested.

I hated that he was being so pragmatic. Why couldn't he panic with me? "Yes, I suppose that could happen," I finally said.

"And in case you didn't notice, I called you earlier to invite you to dinner. How do you feel about Mexican food?"

"I love Mexican food. The cheesier, the better," I said, brightening.

"Great, I'll pick you up at six, if that's okay?" he asked.

I agreed and hung up. He didn't seem bothered by the phone call, but I was. Seeing a dead man's name come up on caller ID made me anxious.

My cell phone rang, and I looked down at it. Lucy.

"Hi, Lucy," I said.

"Hi, Allie, did the kids leave to go back to college?" she asked.

"Yes. Jennifer took Thad and Sarah to the airport, and she will be back to stay the night, and then she'll leave in the morning."

"So what have you found out about Todd Spellman's murder?" she asked, sounding a little greedy for information.

"Not much. They are still waiting on the autopsy, not that we don't already know what he died of. Alec questioned the family, but there wasn't much there. I'm not sure there's much anyone knows at this point," I said.

"Why don't I get to go with you on these interrogations?" she asked. There was a slight whine in her voice.

"Because Alec barely lets me go with him. If I suggested we take you, he'd put his foot down and I wouldn't be allowed to go, either," I pointed out.

She sighed. "I feel so left out."

"Hey, there was something weird that happened a few minutes ago. Someone from Todd Spellman's house called my house phone. His name came up on my caller ID, and when I answered, there was no one on the other end. I can't imagine why anyone in that house would want to call me," I told her.

"What? That's creepy!" she exclaimed. Now that was the reaction I wanted. Why did Alec have to be so sensible?

"I know, right? I mean, why would they call me?"

"I think this calls for an investigation," she exclaimed excitedly.

"Me too. Alec thought it was nothing, but Todd Spellman never called me when he was alive, so why would I get a call from his house now that he's dead?"

"Yeah." There was a pause. "You don't think it's his ghost, do you?" she asked sheepishly.

"No," I said. At least I didn't think it was possible. I didn't believe in ghosts, did I? I thought about it for a second and creeped myself out. No, I did not believe in that sort of thing, and I was not going to start now. "I just have to wonder if something's going on at that house, though."

"All right, when do we go interview them?" she asked.

"Tomorrow. I'll bake a pie, and we can take it over. I have a date with Alec tonight, and I don't want to have to rush to get back in time, so we won't go today," I said.

When my husband had died, I had baked a pie every day for years. It was therapy. Since meeting Alec, I had somehow managed to get out of my daily pie baking habit, so it would be good for me to bake something tomorrow. Even with all the holiday baking, I wasn't baking nearly enough.

Chapter Nine

MY STOMACH GROWLED when the waiter set the bowl of chips and salsa on the table. Would it be rude to slurp down the bowl of salsa, then overturn the chip bowl into my mouth? Probably so. Instead, I opted to take one chip and delicately dip it into the salsa and slowly bring it to my mouth.

"So, anything new on the Todd Spellman case?" I asked after I had chewed and swallowed enough of the chip to not appear rude.

"Just that he was shot with a dear hunting rifle. But we had guessed that would be the case," he said, looking over his menu.

"Have you talked to any more suspects?" I asked, leaving off, *without me.* He had been gracious enough to allow me to go with him to the Spellman's house, and I didn't want to push him.

"No, but I'm going to go to the bank tomorrow to interview some of Todd's employees. Maybe someone knows something there," he said. "How are the cheese enchiladas here?"

"Fabulous. But everything here is fabulous," I said. "What time were you going to go down there?"

Lucy and I were going to drop by the Spellman's with a pie in the morning, but I didn't want to miss sitting in on the interviews at the bank. Someone there had to know something.

He gave me a lopsided grin and reached for a chip. "Well, what time would work for you?"

"You know, I'm thinking early afternoon would be good," I answered, and then realized he was teasing me. I narrowed my eyes at him. "Can I please go with you?"

"I don't know. You're a civilian. What business do you have being there?"

What business? "Well, in case you forgot, someone shot at me. And my son was in danger while he was out there running a race that he had no idea had been canceled on account of a murder."

He chuckled and reached for his glass of water. "Oh, see, now you're taking things personally. I'm sure if the killer really wanted to shoot you, they would have."

I sat back in my chair and gave him a look that would melt steel. "Mr. Blanchard, I've got a mind to tell you off."

"That's Detective Blanchard to you, and I was already planning on the late afternoon. Sound good?"

I smiled. "Perfect."

"Good. What are you ordering?" he asked, still looking at his menu.

"Fajitas. I like the sizzle."

He chuckled again. "I think I'm going to have the carne asada tacos."

"Awesome choice," I said. "And just in time. Here comes the waiter."

The waiter came up and asked for our order just as a Mariachi band entered the dining room. I looked at the waiter and opened my mouth to order fajitas, and the band started up. I glanced at Alec, and then loudly said, "Fajitas."

The waiter leaned in toward me, motioning to his ear. I repeated myself, speaking louder, and he pointed to his ear again. I looked at Alec, who was all smiles, obviously enjoying himself at my expense. I held my hand out for the waiter's order pad, and when he handed it over, I wrote both of our orders down and handed the pad back. He smiled and nodded, then left.

Alec and I ate chips and grinned at each other until the band had passed by us and moved into the adjoining dining room.

"Now you have something to tell your grandchildren," he said. "The day a Mariachi band got the best of Grandma."

"Oh don't say that," I said. "I don't want anyone calling me grandma any time soon."

Alec and I had been seeing each other for over a month, and I still didn't know how he had ended up here in Sandy Harbor. When I had asked over a month ago, before we were dating, he had changed the subject. We should have been past that, so I decided to go for it and ask him directly.

"So, Alec, you never have told me how you ended up here in Sandy Harbor," I said.

He looked at me and then looked down at his place setting. "I guess you could say I needed a change of pace."

"Why?" I asked simply.

He looked at me. "Because I let my partner die. Brass decided I needed a break for a while, and Sandy Harbor police department agreed to take me."

My mouth dropped open. "I'm sorry."

He gave me a half-smile that didn't reach his eyes. "Sometimes, no matter how good your intentions are, you still end up screwing up."

"What happened?"

"We had a hostage situation," he said, reaching for a chip. "Drug dealers had kidnapped one of their customer's daughters and held her for ransom. My partner decided to go in without adequate backup."

"How is that your fault?" I asked gently.

He let out a heavy sigh. "I was supposed to cover him. But I had told him not to go in. He wouldn't listen. I was busy trying to call for backup, and he ran into the house, where he was shot dead."

I looked steadily at him. "How is that your fault?" I repeated.

He looked away. "He was my partner. It was my job to cover him, and I failed."

"Yes, but Alec, weren't you also doing your job by calling in the situation? And didn't you tell him to wait?" I asked. I failed to see why he thought it was his fault. It was understandable that he would feel bad about it, but he had no reason to blame himself.

"Because covering my partner was more important, and I didn't do it," he said, and picked up his glass of water and took a sip. He wouldn't look at me while he talked.

I watched him for a moment. I didn't want to push, but it seemed he was taking too much responsibility on himself. "Would he have blamed himself if the tables were turned and it was you that died?"

He laughed, but it sounded cold. "That's doubtful. Gordon was green. He had just been promoted to detective, and he thought he knew it all. I warned him to wait for backup, but he was sure he could handle it. He never took responsibility for anything, so, no. He would not blame himself." He looked at me when he said the last part.

I nodded slowly. "Do you think there's a possibility you're being too hard on yourself?" I knew he didn't want to hear that, but it seemed obvious to me.

"He had been married less than a year and had a baby on the way."

His eyes became shiny, and he looked away again.

"I'm sorry," I said.

He turned back toward me. "I understand that you think I'm taking the blame on myself, and you think it isn't justified. But Gordon and I argued a lot. All the time. We had been arguing on the way over to the scene. I swore at him and told him I was getting a new partner. He had pushed me over and over. And in the end, when all was said and done, I still can't be sure I did all I could to keep him from getting killed."

"What do you mean?" I asked him. My heart was breaking for him, and I wanted to understand what he had been through.

"I had told him over and over not to go in. But when he said he was going in and I knew he was really going to do it, I told him to do whatever he wanted. I knew how dangerous it was, and I said screw it, and turned away and made a phone call. A stupid phone call."

"A very important phone call," I pointed out gently. I could feel tears in my own eyes, and I blinked them back.

He snorted. "I shouldn't have turned away."

"Alec," I said and reached my hand out to place it on the back of his. He jerked his hand away.

"Don't. Really. Just don't. Plenty of the guys at the station blamed me. Well I blame me, too. I should never have turned away, and now there's a wife and kid without a husband and father. My superior officer sent me here to get away from the guys that blamed me. They thought I should have been charged with negligence or some other charge and fired. And I agree with them."

I breathed out, hard. I wished I could say something to help, but I knew it would only make things worse.

"I'm sorry," is all I had.

"No, I'm sorry. We're supposed to be having a nice evening, and now I've ruined it." He took a sip of his water, refusing to look at me.

"It's not ruined," I said as our dinners were brought to the table. "This smells delicious."

We needed the distraction. He was intent on blaming himself, and there wasn't much I could do to make him feel better. I wondered if he had ever done any therapy, but I didn't want to bring it up. Perhaps later. At least now things were out in the open. Maybe that would help him to deal with it. Secrets tended to eat you alive, if you let them.

Chapter Ten

IT WAS OFFICIALLY THE Christmas season since Thanksgiving was over, but I loved the fall so much, I decided to bake a distinctly fall Southern pie. Sweet potato pie was one of my favorites when I was a little girl. Similar to pumpkin, but more dense. I always doubled up on spices. You can never use too much cinnamon in a sweet potato pie.

It was still slightly warm when Lucy picked me up at ten. I brought a can of whipped cream, just in case the Spellman's didn't have any. You can't eat sweet potato pie without it. Normally I would make my whipped cream from scratch, but it didn't travel as well as the kind in the can.

"That smells wonderful," Lucy said when I got into her car. "Did you happen to make two of them? I wouldn't mind taking one home with me."

"Somehow I knew you were going to say that, and yes I did. Just for you," I said. "When you drop me off afterward, I'll get it for you."

"You're the best," Lucy said.

It had snowed almost a foot overnight and the snowplow was out doing its thing. I still needed to learn how to love snow.

The snow that came before Christmas was far more tolerable than the snow that fell afterward. How was it that pre-Christmas snow was white and beautiful, but post-Christmas snow was dirty and muddy looking? I had never been able to figure that out.

Lucy pulled into the Spellman's driveway, and the curtains were open in the living room. A small Christmas wreath adorned the front door. We got out of the car and headed up the walk. Alec had told me Todd's funeral had been the previous day, and I wondered if any relatives had come from out of town. I didn't know Todd well enough to feel like I should go to the funeral, but I was sure there had been plenty of people from town that had gone.

The door opened before we could get up on the front step, and Connie Sutter met us. "Good morning," she said, looking warily at me, and then Lucy.

"Good morning, Connie, this is my friend Lucy," I said, introducing them. "I baked a pie for y'all this morning and brought it right over. I know it's still early, but it's sweet potato, and that's a vegetable, so it's healthy and can be eaten in the morning. Right?" Turning on my Southern charm might help us get some information.

She glanced at the pie, then back to me. "Oh, you shouldn't have," she said with what looked like a forced smile. She glanced back over her shoulder and then turned back to me.

We stood on the step looking at each other for a few moments and I was beginning to wonder if she would let us in. I held up the reusable shopping bag I had put the pie in. It had a pretty Thanksgiving scene on the front of it, making it festive and inviting. "It's really very good. My grandmama from Alabama taught me how to bake the old Southern way. I've never had a complaint about my pies." The last part might have been untrue, but I wanted inside the house so we could chat.

Then she smiled genuinely at me. "Please, come in," she said and motioned toward the door.

"Let me cut you a piece of this pie," I said. I could see the kitchen through a pass-through in the casual living room and headed there before she could object.

I ran into her husband Terrence on my way. "Oh hello, Terrence, I brought y'all a sweet potato pie. My grandmama taught me to make them, oh, so many years ago!" I said brightly.

"Oh?" he said sounding surprised but didn't try to keep me from my mission.

"This is my friend Lucy," I said over my shoulder as I passed him. "You don't mind me looking for some plates, do you?" I hoped I wasn't about to get kicked out. There were four pies and two cakes on the kitchen counters. "Oh goodness, I see you're already set for sweet things, aren't you?"

"Yes, the ladies from the church sent most of them home with us yesterday," Connie said, coming to stand in the kitchen doorway.

"I'm sorry. I'm being very forward, aren't I?" There was an ancient-looking wall phone on the wall in Todd's kitchen, and I looked at it suspiciously.

"Oh no. No problem," Terrence said, standing next to his wife. "I haven't had sweet potato pie in years."

"Well then, I'll serve you up a slice. I just know y'all will love it," I said, as I found a stack of paper plates on another countertop.

"Allie makes the best pies," Lucy said.

I turned toward them. "How is Mr. Spellman doing today?"

"He's doing well," Terrence answered. "In fact, he'll be right in, any moment now."

I cut a piece of pie and looked up at the pass-through and there was Mr. Spellman, standing in the living room. I nearly dropped the pie when I saw him. I couldn't recall ever seeing Mr. Spellman standing. He still had a slightly dazed look on his face, but he gave me a little smile and a nod.

"Well, Mr. Spellman, you do look well. Would you like some sweet potato pie?" I asked. I glanced at Lucy, and she looked just as shocked as I was to see him standing there.

Mr. Spellman nodded, and his smile got a little bigger, but he didn't say anything.

"Let me help you," Connie said and came to stand beside me.

She looked distinctly uncomfortable as she got out a tray and some napkins. I couldn't tell what was going on here, but something definitely was.

When I had enough pie cut for everyone, we went into the living room to sit and eat it. It was cool in there, and I wondered if Mr. Spellman was cold. He still hadn't said a word, but he was feeding himself his pie and seemed to be enjoying it.

"This is wonderful pie," Terrence said, licking his lower lip. "Your grandmama did a good job when she taught you to bake."

"Oh yes, she did," I replied. I turned to look at Mr. Spellman. "Mr. Spellman, I'm so sorry for your loss."

I hadn't had a chance to say it before, and I wanted to see what his reaction would be. He simply looked up at me and nodded and went on eating his pie.

"It's such a shame," Terrence said.

"Indeed," Lucy said, still eyeing Mr. Spellman. "He seems to be doing so much better." She nodded at Mr. Spellman.

"There seemed to be a mix up with his medication. We've gotten it straightened out though, and he is doing much better," Connie said, fidgeting with the napkin in her hand.

"Really?" I asked.

"Yes," she said and forced herself to smile. "It seems Todd may have made a mistake on some of the dosages."

"It's all understandable, of course," Terrence jumped in. "Todd was young, and he had a career. I'm sure it was a lot to keep up with. But we'll be taking Dad home with us, and he'll get the best of care."

Dad. He'd referred to him as Dad when Alec and I were here, and I wondered if he was really that close to Mr. Spellman. Something seemed off, but I couldn't put my finger on it. I considered mentioning the phone call I had received, but now that I had seen Mr. Spellman up and about, I wondered if I should. Maybe I needed to talk to Alec about it first.

I leaned in toward Terrence. "Does he talk much?" I whispered.

He looked over at Mr. Spellman. "No, not really. He's said a couple of words here and there, mostly unintelligible. Perhaps his ability to speak will return after some time. I certainly hope so."

I leaned back in my seat and then turned to Connie. "You must be so relieved to be able to take your father home with you."

At this, Connie beamed. "Oh, yes. I really am. I was always a daddy's girl. It was so hard when I moved to Michigan. I wish I had never moved away. Or at least, I wish I had taken Daddy with me."

"I'm sure it was very difficult," I said, nodding.

"What line of work are you two in?" Lucy asked.

"I'm a retired fireman," Terrence said. "I injured my shoulder a couple of years ago and decided it was time to retire. After a hefty settlement from the city, of course." He laughed.

"I bet that was interesting work," I said and then turned to Connie. "What do you do, Connie?"

She gave me a nervous smile. "I'm an interior decorator. I work freelance."

"Oh, how fun is that?" Lucy said. "I always wanted to do something like that, but I just don't seem to have the knack for it."

Connie nodded, looking from Lucy to me, and then at her husband.

"Well, it was nice of you ladies to stop by, but Dad has a doctor's appointment, and we really need to get going," Terrence said, getting to his feet.

"Oh, of course," I said, glancing down at the half-eaten slice of pie on my plate. "We didn't mean to keep you."

"The pie was delicious," Connie said.

"Thank you." I glanced at Lucy. She had finished her pie except for the end crust. Lucy never ate the end crust.

We got to our feet, and Connie took our plates. We started toward the door. "Mr. Spellman, I hope you liked that pie. I made it special for you," I said loudly. I wasn't sure how his hearing was.

Mr. Spellman looked at me and smiled. He made an "mmm" sound and nodded his head.

"Good, I'm so glad," I said. It felt like we were getting the bum's rush, but we had dropped by unannounced, so I couldn't blame them. Unfortunately, we didn't get much additional information, but the fact that Mr. Spellman was now up and about was surprising.

When we were back in the car, Lucy asked, "What did you think?"

"I'm not sure," I said buckling my seatbelt. "I think it's pretty bizarre that Mr. Spellman can suddenly walk and feed himself. You saw how he was last week."

"Exactly," she said, pulling away from the curb. "Why didn't you mention the phone call?"

"I don't know. Something told me not to. I'll talk to Alec about it. Something funny's going on there."

Chapter Eleven

"OKAY, SO I HAVE SOMETHING to tell you," I said to Alec. We were in his car, on the way to the Bank of Maine to question the employees there. Hopefully, someone would give us a clue as to why someone would want to kill Todd.

"Go on," he said, pulling into the bank parking lot.

"Lucy and I went to visit Todd Spellman's family yesterday. I baked them a fantastic sweet potato pie that got raves all the way around," I said.

He sighed. "Allie, why do you insist on running around behind my back and investigating?" he asked as he pulled into a parking spot.

"What? I'm not doing anything behind your back. I'm simply going on fact-finding missions. I tell you everything I find out," I said.

He turned toward me. "Allie, please. This can be dangerous. Why don't you let me do the investigating?"

"Don't you want to know what happened?" I asked him.

"Sure. Go ahead. Tell me what you found out."

I didn't like his tone, but I decided to let it slide. "Mr. Spellman was out of his wheelchair and walking. He was fairly clear-eyed and was almost like a completely different person. It was weird."

His brow furrowed. "And did you ask what had happened?"

"Connie said Todd had made a mistake on his medications and was giving him too much. They had taken him to the doctor and got his meds straightened out," I said.

"Okay. So his meds are straightened out now. Why is that weird?" he asked. He still had both of his hands on the steering wheel.

"What do you mean, why is that weird? He was practically a zombie before. I had to feed him a piece of pie at the Turkey Trot," I said, exasperated. Why did he always have to remain calm and level headed about everything?

"And did Mr. Spellman have anything to say?"

"No, apparently he isn't talking much," I said. "But they're hopeful he will speak again soon."

He nodded. "Okay, I've got some people to interview. Let's go," he said and opened his door and got out.

I got out of the car. "Don't you think it's suspicious?" I asked, hurrying to his side. "Especially after that phone call I got the other day?"

He shrugged. "I don't know. It isn't good to connect things that aren't connected. Or things you aren't sure are connected. I've noted it, and will keep it in mind."

I sighed. For a detective, he wasn't very suspicious. I hurried to keep up with him. He held the door for me to go inside the bank.

Jane Marshall was the assistant manager, and she met us at the door. "Good morning, Detective, and uh, Allie. There's a small office you can use over here," she said, pointing to an open door. I knew Jane from when her son Jake was in little league with Thad. She seemed nice enough, but I was going to pay more attention to her since she was a possible suspect now.

She showed us to the office, and we took seats behind the small desk.

"So, Allie, I didn't know you worked with the police department?" she asked as she sat in the chair across from us.

I stared at her, not sure what to say. No one had come right out and asked me that before. Most people we had talked to had just assumed I was supposed to be there.

"Jane, can you tell me about your relationship with Todd Spellman?" Alec asked, ignoring her question.

I tried not to smile. He was good. Very good.

"Oh. My relationship?" Jane asked, sitting up straighter. "What do you mean? He was my boss. That's all."

Huh. *Defensive much, Jane?*

Alec had his pen and notebook out and was scribbling in it. How did he do that so fast?

"Did you enjoy working for him?" Alec asked without looking up.

"Well, sure. I mean, I guess so. You know how it is. Sometimes things can get tense. Different personalities and all," she said, fidgeting.

Alec stopped writing and looked up at her. After a moment, he asked, "Can you expand on that? The different, tense personalities part?"

Jane's eyes got bigger. "Well, it's just that Todd was very particular in how things were done. He didn't want to leave loose ends on anything. He was a professional, I guess you could say."

"He was a jerk?" I supplied. I wanted to see if the things Bob had said about Todd were true.

She gave me a smile that didn't reach her eyes. "He could be very demanding. If you didn't get your work done on time, he would sometimes lose it. I mean, screaming lose it."

"I see," Alec said and made a note.

Jane's eyes went to the notebook. "What are you writing?"

"Details. Was there anyone that had a real problem with Todd?" he asked, pulling the notebook closer to himself.

"Yes. George Dillard. He's the owner of the Gas and Go on Third. He came in a month or so ago and applied for a loan. His gasoline tanks had sprung a leak, and he needed the money to have them repaired. He didn't get the loan, and he was mad." Being able to shine a little light on someone else seemed to make her happy. She leaned back in her seat and relaxed.

"Did Todd make the decision on that?" Alec asked, making more notes.

"No, it has to go up the chain. But Todd can give his opinion on whether he thinks it's a good idea to make the loan, and he told the loan department in Bangor that he didn't think George was a good risk. Then he *told* George that he told the loan department that. George freaked," she said.

"Why would he do that?" Alec asked, looking puzzled. "It seems like that would be confidential between him and the loan department. And foolish to say it."

She shrugged. Her graying hair was long and curled, and she pushed it back over her shoulder. I had always envied her hair, and I still did, even though it was graying now. The gray made her look distinctive.

"Todd was that way sometimes. You never knew what was going to come out of his mouth. When our lead teller, Patty Guzman, was pregnant with twins, he told her she was getting fat, and she needed to lose weight or her husband would leave her. He *knew* she was pregnant. We had had a baby shower for her here at the bank. She went home crying."

"Sounds like Todd really was a jerk," I said. How could I have thought he was such a wonderful person? It just goes to show you that people aren't always what they portray themselves to be.

She nodded, knowingly.

"Can you elaborate on George Dillard freaking?" Alec asked. I glanced at him. I couldn't believe he said that with a straight face.

She leaned forward in her chair. "He started screaming that Todd was a jerk. Well, jerk was the nicest word he used to describe him. It was the noon rush hour, and we had a line of customers out to the front door, and George was in Todd's office with the door open. And screaming. I was afraid he was going to have a stroke. George isn't getting any younger. His face was beet red."

Alec seemed to consider her for a moment before writing in his notebook. "Is there anything else you think we should know?"

She shrugged. "Nothing comes to mind. Just that Todd wasn't who you thought he was."

"Fine. Thank you for your time. Please send someone else in," he said.

She left, and Bob Payne appeared at the door. "I don't have anything to tell you that I haven't already told you," he said.

"Fine, come on in and have a seat," Alec said.

I smiled at him.

Bob made a low groaning sound and came in and sat down. "This is a waste of time."

"Can you tell me if there was anyone that had problems with Todd Spellman?" Alec asked, ignoring his comment.

"Like I said before, Todd was a jerk, and no one that really knew him liked him."

"So you're saying that you had problems with him?" Alec asked, not looking up from his notebook.

"Look, I didn't say that. I did my best to get along with the guy. He was my boss. But he had a way about him. He had one side he showed to certain people, and another he showed to others," Bob said. I could see small beads of sweat breaking out on his forehead.

"Did you kill Todd Spellman?" Alec asked.

"What?" Bob said, his eyes bulging. "No! No, I never killed anyone. I swear. How can you think that?"

Alec smiled. "Calm down, Bob. No one's accusing you of anything. It's just a question I need to ask."

Alec was having fun with Bob. I hadn't seen this side of him before. It was all I could do to keep from laughing. Poor Bob didn't find it humorous though. One of those small beads of sweat had grown into a large bead and trickled down the side of his face. Alec had mercy on Bob a few minutes later and excused him.

After the fifth person had been interviewed, I began to have regrets about insisting I come with Alec. I was getting tired and hungry, and everyone seemed to have the same story about Todd. He was a jerk. Shocking. He was always taking his ailing father everywhere with him and had seemed so engaged when he spoke to anyone.

"I hated Todd," Patty Guzman said, and tears sprang to her eyes. "He was always making fun of me. He said I needed to shave. My face. Can I help it if I have hormone issues? I do the best I can to get rid of it."

I handed her a Kleenex from the box on the desk and refrained from looking at Alec. She was number ten.

"I understand that he could be a difficult person to work for," Alec said. "Can you think of anyone that might have wanted to hurt him?"

"Everyone!" she blurted out, dabbing at her eyes. "He was a terrible person. He called me three days after I gave birth and wanted to know when I was coming back to work. It was a cesarean!"

I felt my eyes go wide. I was thankful I had never worked for Todd. I might have slugged him.

"I see," Alec said and made more notes. He must have been close to getting writers' cramp by that time.

Patty was our last interviewee. When we finished, I heaved a sigh of relief.

"Wow," I whispered as we headed to Alec's SUV.

"Wow is right. Like I told you, you never know a person like you think you do," he said.

I got in the car and leaned back. We had a lot to process.

Chapter Twelve

"HERE YOU GO. YOU TWO enjoy yourselves," the waitress said, setting two baskets of popcorn shrimp and fries, and a breadbasket down on the table.

My stomach growled loudly as I reached for the breadbasket. "Sorry," I said and chuckled.

"Food always tastes best when you're hungry," he said.

"That it does," I answered. "So what do you make of what everyone said today?"

He gave a quick shake of his head. "That Todd was something else. But lots of people are mean and ugly, and it doesn't get them killed."

"I guess it depends on if you come across the wrong person when you're being mean. That can get you killed," I said. And Todd had done it. I shuddered when I thought about it. It could have been someone I've dealt with at the grocery store, or the bank, or any other place.

"That it can," he said. "Hopefully we'll get something back from the lab in the next couple of days. We couldn't come up with any clear fingerprints, but maybe there's something else on the materials we sent to them."

The shrimp was steaming hot, and the best I had ever tasted. Alec was right about food tasting better when you're hungry. Stan's Crab Shack was filled almost to capacity. The Christmas shopping season was upon us and shoppers were taking a few minutes to rest in between stores to get something to eat.

"So tell me, how's the blog coming? I haven't heard you mention it in a while," he said.

I looked up from my food. "Well," I said slowly. "I think I might be done with it."

He raised his eyebrows at me. "What do you mean, done?"

"I don't know. I think Lucy might be right. It might be keeping me in a state of grieving. I've been thinking about it for a while now. The only thing is, I'm not sure how to end it. I haven't written anything substantial in several weeks, and I feel like I'm abandoning people in their time of need." There. I had said it. I felt guilty about ending the blog.

"Well, I can see how you might feel that way. After all, it's been eight years, right? That's a long time to do anything," he said, sitting back in his seat. "Maybe you should take the time to think it over?"

I nodded. "I suppose I can. But if the truth be told, I do feel like it's time to end it. I've made a lot of online friends through the blog. I feel like people need an explanation, and I'm not sure how to give it."

Maybe I had abandonment issues. But it felt like walking away from people that needed me. How could I do that?

"Maybe you could let them know ending it is a part of the process? Moving on is a part of the process, right? It isn't healthy for anyone to stay in grief indefinitely," he observed.

"True," I said. He was right. I knew he was. I needed to find a way to get over feeling like I was letting people down.

"Hi, Allie!" Someone called from across the room.

We both looked up and saw Rebecca Holding waving at me. She had her six-year-old daughter, Sarah, in tow. I waved back as they wove their way around people to get to us. I got to my feet and gave them each a hug in turn and introduced them to Alec. I had babysat Rebecca when she was Sarah's age, and Thad had dated her sister in high school. Small towns.

"I don't want to interrupt you two, but I saw you over here and thought I'd say hi. So hi!" she said and giggled.

"Hi," I said and looked at the shopping bags on her arm. "Looks like you're getting your Christmas shopping done early."

"Oh, I try to every year, but it seems like I always forget something and end up in a rush on Christmas Eve," she said. "Say, I heard you were at the Turkey Trot when Todd Spellman was shot. Wasn't he the manager at the Bank of Maine?"

"Yes, he was," I said and introduced her to Alec. "We were both there, and so was Thad. He was visiting with his new girlfriend for Thanksgiving."

"Oh, tell him hello next time you see him. That must have been terrifying," she said, shaking her head.

"Yes, it was. Poor Todd," I answered.

She glanced over her shoulder quickly and then turned back to me. "Listen, Allie, I don't mean to be a gossip or a snoop, but I heard Rudy Gallo was over at the Brass Rail, laughing it up over Todd's death. Not that I would ever go to a bar, mind you, but occasionally my husband Bill stops off and has a beer there. He said Rudy said that Todd got what he deserved." She leaned in toward me. "Honestly, I don't think anyone deserves to be murdered, but if someone did, it would have to be Todd. He could be the nicest person or the meanest, depending on his mood."

It took everything I had not to give Alec a look. "You know, I never experienced that with Todd, but I've heard the same thing. Did Rudy give any reason why he thought it was funny that Todd was murdered?"

"He told Bill that Todd had refused to give him a home loan. Laughed at his credit score, he did," she said. "I guess he's still bitter."

"Wow. Yeah, I can see where that would make a person mad. But mad enough to murder someone?" I asked.

She shrugged. "Who knows with people these days? Not that I actually think he did it, mind you."

"That's true," I agreed. "It's going to take some time for the police to sort this thing out."

She smiled at me. "Well, I've got to go. I think my order should be ready. I'm beat from all this shopping, and I'm going to take an order to go. Bill is at home, and he has got to be starving by now."

"I'll see you around, Rebecca. You too, Sarah," I said as they left.

I whipped my head back to look at Alec so fast you'd have thought I'd have gotten whiplash. "Small town!" I whispered.

A small smile played on Alec's lips. "Small towns are very different from larger ones, aren't they?"

I nodded. "I don't know how I missed the fact that Todd was hated by so many people. He always seemed so nice."

"Some people are masters at making you think what they want you to think about them. Who is Rudy Gallo, and do you have any idea why he wouldn't like Todd Spellman?" he asked. "Besides being laughed at for having a low credit score? That sounds kind of flimsy."

"Rudy owns the plumbing supply store on Main Street. You have to take small-town gossip with a grain of salt sometimes. Are we going to go talk to him?"

Alec had that pen and notebook out again. I swear it was attached to him somewhere and appeared the second he thought about making a note. He wrote Rudy's name in the book and closed it.

"I would imagine I will at some point," he said. He looked across the room and narrowed his eyes.

I turned in the direction he was looking and saw Sam Bailey had just entered the restaurant. Alec hadn't mentioned having any issues with Sam, but if I had to guess by the look on his face, he did.

Sam looked in our direction, waved, and made his way over. He was still in his too-tight uniform, and he maneuvered around the people waiting to pick up takeout meals at the register. Sam had been the chief of police for fifteen years, but he still wore a uniform like the rest of the officers in patrol cars. I wasn't sure why, as the uniforms didn't look terribly comfortable, but I couldn't remember him ever wearing anything else.

"Alec," he said, nodding at him, then turned to me. "Hello, Allie, how are you doing?"

I smiled at him. Sam had always been pleasant to me. Jennifer and his daughter had been best friends in junior high but had drifted apart in high school. "I'm fine, Sam, how are you?"

"Very good. The weather has changed, and it's a little warmer than it should be for this time of year," he said. He glanced at Alec but kept speaking to me. "How's that blog you're writing? It's a blog, isn't it? I seem to forget what people are doing these days."

"Yes, it's a blog on grief," I said. "And it's doing well. I've enjoyed writing it."

He nodded, his eyes still on me. "You know, I've had some reports that a woman police officer has been accompanying my detective on interviews, but I haven't had a woman police officer since Michelle Smith retired last year. I'm not sure who they could be talking about." He looked at me meaningfully.

I sensed Alec stiffen, more than saw it happen. I smiled at Sam again. "That's odd, isn't it?" My heart pounded, and sweat suddenly slicked my palms, but I wasn't going to give Alec away.

He smiled back at me. "I'll have to check into that." He glanced at Alec.

"How did you like the popcorn balls I dropped by the station last month, Sam?" I asked. Sam had a sweet tooth as big as his head, and maybe a reminder of my wares would smooth things over. It was always at the back of my mind that Alec might get into trouble by allowing me to ride along with him, and it looked like this might be the day.

"They were the best popcorn balls I've ever tasted," he said with a smile. "You have a way with sweets."

That's what I thought. I was a crack dealer, and Sam was my junkie. "You know, I've had you on my mind, Sam. I was thinking about making you a batch of persimmon cookies. If I may say so, no one makes persimmon cookies like I do. I'll have to bring you a batch," I said. The way to a man's heart is through his stomach, and if I could get him to feel favorably toward me and my sugary wares, maybe it would keep Alec out of trouble.

Sam gave me a genuine smile. "Well, that's real thoughtful of you, Allie. I would appreciate that."

"Well, you be expecting to see me stop by real soon with those cookies, then," I said cheerfully.

"I will. I've got to be going now," he said and straightened up. He glanced at Alec again. "Alec," he said, and then sauntered off.

We both watched him go. I turned to Alec once he was at the cash register, giving his order, and out of earshot.

I sighed loudly. "I'm sorry. I knew there was a chance you would get in trouble for letting me tag along."

He shook his head. "No, it's my fault. I shouldn't have allowed it."

"Maybe persimmon cookies will get you off the hook," I said and smiled at him. But he wasn't cheering up. Something told me he was having trouble at work beyond someone complaining about me tagging along, and he didn't want to talk about it.

We finished our meal, keeping conversation to lighter topics.

Chapter Thirteen

THE NEXT MORNING, I baked persimmon cookies after my run on the treadmill. It was time to call it winter and call it quits for running outside. The previous three days, my nose had frozen so solidly, I had been sure it would snap off if I touched it. I had finally settled on running a marathon in Sanford in May. It would be a bit of a drive, but Alec and I could make a weekend of it.

I had frozen persimmon pulp two months ago when the fruit was ripe and had thawed it in the fridge overnight. I was going to outdo myself and make twelve dozen cookies. Sam Bailey was going to get three dozen. Hopefully that would keep him happy for a while, and he wouldn't interfere with me tagging along with Alec to talk to people. I had visions of having to bribe Sam with baked goods every time I wanted to ride along with Alec, but that was a small price to pay.

I was giving Alec a dozen cookies, plus a couple of dozen for the other officers, and I was going to take some to Connie and Terrence and Mr. Spellman. I wanted to check up on Mr. Spellman anyhow and see how he was doing.

Persimmon cookies were some of my all-time fall favorites. I added chopped walnuts and raisins as well as a hefty helping of spices. The cookies were so soft and moist, they were almost like tiny cakes.

I had an assembly line going with the cookie sheets. My husband, Thaddeus had put in a double oven for me when we remodeled our kitchen ten years ago, so with the cookie sheets turned long ways, I had eight dozen cookies baking at once. Don't mess with me, I'm a professional.

I texted Alec while the cookies baked.

Hey, I'll be over around 10:30 with persimmon cookies
Maybe you shouldn't come?
Why? I told Sam I was bringing him some cookies
I don't want to get him started up
It will be fine. See you at 10:30.

Alec needed to relax. I would butter Sam up, and all would be fine. He just needed to trust my Southern charm.

I PULLED INTO THE POLICE station parking lot at 10:32. Perfect. I had packed the cookies in wax paper-lined Christmas gift boxes, and I got them out of the trunk of my car and headed in.

"Early Christmas present, fellas," I said to Yancey Tucker and George Feeney. Their desks sat behind a counter that separated the lobby from the rest of the police station.

"Wow, thanks, Allie," George said, jumping up and taking the box from me. "I don't know what it is, but I can smell it through the box."

"Persimmon Cookies," I said. "Okay if I go back to see Alec?"

"Sure," Yancey said, not looking at me. He had joined George, and each already had a cookie in both of their hands.

I hummed jingle bells as I headed down the hall toward Alec's office. I couldn't wait to put my Christmas tree up and put the lights on the house.

Before I could make it to the end of the hall, Sam Bailey stepped out from a doorway and looked at me. He didn't say a word.

"Hi, Sam, persimmon cookies, as promised. I baked a batch special, just for you," I said, and held one of the boxes out to him. I cranked up the Southern accent and charm and gave him my best smile.

He reluctantly gave me a tight-lipped smile in return and took the box from me. He couldn't resist my cookies. No one could.

"Thanks, Allie. I bet these are great," he said, looking at the box.

"They are. I put extra spices in them. That's what makes them special." I slipped past him, hoping he wouldn't say anything about me riding along with Alec.

"Where are you headed?" he asked.

Dang it. "Oh, just taking some cookies to Alec," I said, holding up the remaining box. "He loves my cookies."

Sam didn't say anything else, and I continued down the hall and knocked on Alec's door. I could feel Sam watching me, and I had to resist the temptation to turn around and look at him. Just play it cool, I told myself.

"Come in," Alec called from the other side of the door.

I opened the door and slipped inside, shutting it behind me. I gave him a big smile. "Hey, I made you some persimmon cookies, as promised."

He gave me a half-smile. "You shouldn't be here."

"Nonsense, I bribed Sam with cookies. It's fine," I whispered. The walls in the police station were thin, and I was sure Sam was still out in the hall.

He shook his head. "You are incorrigible."

I leaned over and gave him a quick kiss. "These are good with coffee." I opened the box, and the smell of cloves wafted up.

"Wow, those do smell good," he admitted and took one.

"So tell me, did you get the lab reports back?" I asked, sitting in the visitor's chair and helping myself to a cookie.

He swallowed and nodded. "The gun was a hunting rifle, which we knew. Whoever the shooter was, they were an ace marksman. Shot him through the heart. He died instantly."

"Wow," I said. "Then why didn't they hit you or me when they were shooting at us?"

He shrugged. "That's a good question. Maybe because they didn't want to kill us. But then you have to wonder why shoot at us at all? It doesn't make sense."

"And what about fingerprints on anything removed from the scene?" I was starting to sound more and more like a real detective, and I was proud of myself.

"Nothing. Not one. I was hoping they could come up with something at the lab, but no such luck," he said and took a sip of his coffee.

"Anything new on who else hated Todd? Other than everyone at his place of employment?" I asked, sitting back in my chair. I was tempted to open Alec's office door and see if Sam Bailey was still out there, but then I'd have to explain why I was suspicious. We kept whispering instead.

"No one new, yet. But the medical examiner's office came back with something interesting," he said.

"What?" I asked excitedly. "Tell me."

He chuckled. "You must be a lot of fun on Christmas morning," he said. "There were scratches on his chest, and one on his neck. He also had a faint bruise on his left jawline and a couple more on his chest."

"Scratches? What kind of scratches?"

"He must have had a scuffle with someone," he said.

"I didn't notice a bruise on Thanksgiving morning," I said, trying to remember back.

"The scratches had nearly healed up, and the bruise was faded. Do you know if he was seeing anyone? No one at the bank mentioned he had a significant other," he said.

I shook my head. "I have no idea. I didn't know him well at all."

"Well, it's something to look into," he said, and opened the file folder he had in front of him and flipped through the papers in it.

"Is that the file on Todd?" I asked and bit into my cookie.

He nodded. "Yes, it is."

I leaned forward. "Are there pictures of him in there? You know, dead pictures?"

He looked up at me. "Yes, there are. Were you interested in seeing them?"

I sat back in my chair. "No. I do not want to see pictures."

He smirked at me and went back to the file. "Did you ever figure out who called you from Todd Spellman's residence?" he asked without looking up.

"No. I have no idea," I said. "But I baked them some cookies and I'm going to drop them by. Just to see how things are going."

"Allie, I want you to go easy on them. They just had a traumatic death in the family."

I gasped. "I do understand about grief," I said indignantly.

"I know, I know. Sorry," he said. "I just don't want Sam Bailey to get any complaints."

"Okay, I understand," I said. Sam Bailey could become a problem. Baked sugary bribes or not. "Are you going to do any investigating today?" I whispered the last part.

"Some, but I'm going to do it on my own. Let's play it cool for a while, okay?"

"Got it." Sam Bailey couldn't do anything about Lucy and me investigating on our own.

Chapter Fourteen

"HELLO, CONNIE, I HOPE I'm not disturbing you," I said when the Spellman's door opened. "I was baking persimmon cookies for a friend, and I thought y'all might like some, too. They're my grandmama's special recipe."

I held the box out, smiling brightly.

Connie may have been a little surprised to see me. She stood there looking at me, her eyes wide. "Oh, that's so sweet of you," she finally said. "Thank you."

She still stood there without taking the box or inviting me in.

"If it's okay with you, I'll just put these in the kitchen for you," I said, and gently pushed past her. "How is Mr. Spellman doing today?" I said over my shoulder as I headed to the kitchen. I was taking liberties here, but as long as no one stopped me, I wasn't going to keep going.

"Oh, he's doing well," she said as she hurried to keep up with me. "We weren't expecting company, please excuse the mess."

On the living room floor were open boxes of paperwork and books. Piles of paperwork covered the top of the coffee table and end table, and there was a messy stack of books in the middle of the floor.

"Oh, that's okay, don't you worry about a thing. I know when I'm going through things, I tend to spread stuff around, too. I expect it's a lot, going through things and getting the house packed up," I said sympathetically. I set the box of cookies on the kitchen counter and opened it up. "Don't they smell heavenly?" I asked, giving her my best smile.

"Why, yes, yes they do," she agreed and glanced nervously over her shoulder.

"Is everything okay, Connie?" I asked. I hoped she would say something that would give me a clue about the murder. If she knew anything at all.

She smiled. "Yes, of course, why wouldn't it be?"

"Oh, no reason," I said, shaking my head. I didn't want to blow it. "Is Mr. Spellman around? I just know he'd love these cookies."

"He's napping," she said. We were still standing in the kitchen. It didn't look like I was going to be asked to have a seat.

There was an uncomfortable silence with both of us standing there, looking at each other.

"Connie, why don't you try one of these cookies? They're so moist, they'll make you cry," I said, holding the box up for her to see from where she stood.

"No, thank you. I've just eaten, and I couldn't eat another bite. But I do appreciate you bringing them by. Perhaps after dinner this evening, we'll all try one," she said.

"Is Terrence around? I bet he'd like one," I suggested. I knew I was pushing it, but I didn't care.

"No, he went out for a paper," she said, still standing and looking at me.

Now what? She wasn't giving an inch, and I needed a foot if I was ever going to figure out who killed Todd Spellman.

"Connie, I just wanted to express my condolences on the loss of your brother again. I'm sure there are a lot of people mourning him. I didn't know him well personally, but I would imagine a man as caring as he was would have a significant other. I feel terribly for her, whoever she is," I said.

Connie's body language said she wasn't thrilled to have me paying her another visit.

"I think he mentioned there was someone he was seeing last time I spoke to him on the phone, but I never met her," she said and gave me a tired sigh.

"Oh, that's a shame. I'm sure he would have liked to have introduced you both," I said, nodding sympathetically.

"Listen, Allie, I do appreciate you bringing the cookies by, but we would like our privacy," she said flatly.

"Oh, of course. I understand completely. Did you ever get a chance to take a look at my blog? The one on grief?"

She breathed out heavily. "I'm going to have to ask you to leave now, Allie. Thank you for all your help."

I was shocked. No one had ever asked me to leave their home before. Well, except for my first boyfriend's mama. But Betty Jean Stuart was a snob, and I didn't do anything to deserve to be asked to leave.

"Oh, I see. Yes, well, I understand. You just give me a call if you need anything," I said, and made a beeline to the front door.

I didn't want to be tossed out on my ear, so I thought it best to go willingly.

I could hear her footsteps behind me, and when I got to the front door, she reached past me. "Oh," I said when she brushed up against my back and opened the door for me. If she got any closer, she would bump me out the door and off the front step.

I took a step down onto the bottom step and turned to say goodbye when the door slammed in my face.

Well!

Having a door slammed in my face was a first for me. Okay, a second. Betty Jean was a door slammer. I stared at it for a few seconds, trying to regain my composure, and then went to my car.

Within eleven minutes, I was on Lucy's doorstep.

"Hey, let's go to the Cup and Bean and get a coffee," I said when she answered the door.

She smiled, looking at me curiously. "Why? What's up?"

"Why do you say that?" I innocently asked.

"Because I know you too well. Let me get my coat, and I'll be right out," she said.

THE CUP AND BEAN WAS bustling for being this late in the morning. I ordered a cinnamon chestnut latte, and Lucy got a holiday spice cappuccino. I turned and surveyed the room and saw old Mr. Winters sitting at a table in the corner near the front window, reading the morning paper.

"Come on," I said to Lucy, and we headed toward the back of the coffee shop.

"So? Spill it. What do you know?" she asked.

I shrugged. "Honestly, not that much," I whispered and glanced at Mr. Winters.

She looked in his direction, then turned back to me and shrugged.

"I just can't understand who would want to kill poor Todd Spellman," I said in a slightly louder than conversational tone of voice. "He was such a good and kind person."

Lucy narrowed her eyes at me. "Oh, yes. Yes, he was," she said, catching on. "He was always such a giver. It's a shame that someone could mercilessly kill someone like him."

We both glanced at Mr. Winters, but he was still reading his paper.

"You know, I can't imagine who it could be. Everyone knows what a wonderful person Todd was," I said.

"Oh, I agree. Maybe it was just some unlucky deer hunter that missed his mark," Lucy said.

I tsk-tsked a little, but Mr. Winters wasn't biting. That was odd. Mr. Winters owned a pair of fancy supersonic hearing aids, and he usually volunteered whatever information he had. I sighed and looked at Lucy.

"Come on," I said, and we picked up our coffees and headed to Mr. Winters' table.

"Good morning, Mr. Winters," I said. "Can we share your table?"

Mr. winters continued reading his paper. I looked at Lucy.

"Mr. Winters?" Lucy said loudly. "Mr. Winters?"

Mr. Winters looked up and jumped a little. "Oh, hello, ladies. Didn't see you there."

"Good Morning," I said. "Can we share your table? It's getting crowded in here." There were plenty of empty tables, including the one we had just vacated, but that was a minor detail.

"Eh? I can't hear you!" he said loudly, tilting his head toward me.

"Can we sit?" I said loudly and pointed to one of the empty chairs at his table.

He reached for his ear and touched his hearing aid. "I turned my hearing aid off to save the battery. Those things are expensive."

Lucy pulled a chair out and sat down, and I followed her lead. What good were supersonic hearing aids if you turned them off?

"How are you, Mr. Winters?" I asked.

"Oh, fine, fine," he said. "Say, have you heard anything new about Todd Spellman's murder?"

"No, not much at all," I said and forced myself not to look at Lucy.

"Well, I heard Rudy Gallo did it. He's a deer hunter, you know. He hated Todd because he wouldn't give him a home loan. Said Todd laughed at his credit score."

"I didn't know he was a deer hunter, but a lot of people in these parts are deer hunters," I said. It didn't make a lot of sense to me, but maybe Rudy had a temper, and being laughed at was just too much for him.

"I'm not buying it," Lucy said. "I mean, laughing at someone isn't reason enough to kill over. Maybe it's reason enough to punch someone, but not kill them."

"Well, there's also the matter of Rudy's underage daughter," Mr. Winter said.

"What? What matter?" I asked, leaning in.

"Rudy has a eighteen-year-old daughter, and word has it that Todd had his eye on her. She's a looker, that one. A cheerleader at the high school," Mr. Winters said and folded over the paper he had been reading.

My heart skipped a beat. Had Rudy's daughter been responsible for the scratches found on Todd's body?

"Now that's reason enough to kill someone over," Lucy said, nodding.

"It certainly is," I said. If a thirty-something man had been stalking Jennifer when she was eighteen, I'd murder someone, too. Eighteen is an adult, but no way would I have allowed it since Jennifer had turned eighteen her senior year, and according to Mr. Winters, Rudy's daughter was a cheerleader still in high school.

"And don't forget, in September, someone went over to Todd Spellman's house and busted out all of his windows," he said, nodding his head. "Every one of them, from what I hear."

"I never heard that," I said. "Lucy, did you hear that one?"

"Oh, you know what? I think I did hear about that. I forgot all about it," she said, her brow furrowed in thought.

"Really? That could be kind of important. How could you not remember that?" I asked her.

She shrugged. "That was over two months ago. Besides, who says that has anything to do with his murder?"

"Because I think someone busting out every window in someone's house probably shows a lot of rage. Enough rage to want to kill that person," I said. I thought that would be obvious, but I guess I was wrong.

"Seems that way to me, too," Mr. Winters said.

"How do you two know about this?" I asked. I needed facts if I was going to present something to Alec.

"Well, I don't really recall," Mr. Winters said, stirring his coffee.

"I can't remember either," Lucy said. "Oh, no, wait. I think it was Diana Bowen. Yes, that's it. She had gone to a Chamber of Commerce meeting, and everyone was talking about it."

Great. Diana was dead, and Mr. Winters had no idea who he'd heard it from. These two were never going to be detective material.

Chapter Fifteen

"SURPRISE!" I WHISPERED, poking my head around Alec's office door.

He jumped and squealed a little, then tried to cover it up with a cough. "What are you doing here, Allie?"

"I just stopped in to say hello. Can I get a hello from you?" I asked, offended.

"You could have knocked," he said. He gave me a frown instead of a hello.

"It's not like I barged in. Your door was open a crack," I pointed out. "I would think that I would rate a little happier greeting."

"Sorry," he said. He stood up and leaned over his desk and gave me a quick peck on the cheek.

"Is something wrong?" I asked as he sat down again.

"No, nothing," he said quietly. "Well, actually, yes. The police chief doesn't want you riding along with me. It's not like I can blame him. It's a tremendous risk for you, and I knew better than to allow it."

"He doesn't have to know," I pointed out. By his demeanor, I suspected Sam Bailey had said more than what Alec was letting

107

on, but I decided not to press him. I didn't want to cause trouble for him.

"No, Allie, no more riding along. I just can't have it. It's too risky," he said, looking at his computer screen. We sat in silence for a few minutes. He didn't even look in my direction. It kind of hurt my feelings that he was ignoring me, but I decided to chalk it up to pressure from the job.

I reached over and closed his office door. "I found out a couple of things that are interesting," I whispered.

He glanced at me. "Why are you investigating on your own?"

"I wasn't investigating. At least not in the traditional sense. Lucy and I ran into Mr. Winters at the Cup and Bean. Mr. Winters said that back in September, someone broke out all the windows in Todd Spellman's house. All of them. I would think he would have filed a police report."

Alec glanced at me again and then started typing on his keyboard. He shook his head. "I'm not finding a report. You're right. I would think he would have reported that. His house has a lot of large windows. It had to cost him a small fortune to replace them."

"It would be hard to convince the insurance agency that it was an act of nature," I pointed out.

"For sure," he said, still looking at his computer screen.

"I found out something else, too. It seems there's an eighteen-year-old girl that Todd might have had his eye on before he was murdered."

He looked at me. "Who? And how do you know this?"

"Rudy Gallo's daughter. Mr. Winters told me," I said, sitting back in my chair. It was freezing in his office, and now I regretted putting my hair up. "She's still in high school, by the way."

"How would Mr. Winters know this?"

I shrugged. "He's not big on details sometimes. He said he couldn't remember who told him."

He began twirling a pencil between his fingers, deep in thought. "That could be why Rudy is so happy that Todd was dead."

"That could be why Todd's dead," I added.

He slowly nodded his head. "I suppose that could be."

"So? Good info?"

He looked at me again. "I don't want you doing anything with this, do you understand? I need you to stay out of this. And don't talk to anyone about it."

"Well," I said slowly. "Remember, I said Lucy was with me when Mr. Winters told me. So she already knows."

He sighed loudly and rolled his eyes. "Is anything a secret in this town?"

"Oh, I'm sure there are plenty of secrets in this town. It's just that sometimes they leak out."

"HI, HONEY, IT'S MAMA. How are you?" I asked when Jennifer answered the phone.

"Hi, Mama, I'm fine," she answered.

"Honey, the reason I'm calling is, I was wondering, do you know a girl from high school with the last name of Gallo?"

"Sure. There's Trisha, Sandy, and Amy. Trisha and Sandy are sisters to each other and cousins to Amy. Why?" she asked. I could hear water running in the background.

"Are you taking a bath?" I asked.

"Yes, I am," she said.

"It's dangerous having the phone in the bathtub," I said. "Why do you insist on living dangerously like this?"

She sighed loudly. I could imagine her rolling her eyes at me. "Mom, I'm going to finish my bath. I'll talk to you later."

"No, no!" I said. "Which one of those girls is a cheerleader and eighteen?"

"Why do you want to know?" she asked. Kids. They never answer a question without asking a question.

"Which one?" I asked.

"Amy and Sandy are both a year behind me in school, so are probably both eighteen. But only Amy is a cheerleader."

"Have I met her? The name sounds familiar. I know her father because of the plumbing shop, but what about her?"

"Yes, she came to the '80's party I had at the roller skating rink last Halloween. She dressed like Pat Benatar."

"Awesome, honey. Thank you. Be careful with that phone."

I hung up before she could ask me any more questions. Then I trotted down the hall to her bedroom and looked over her bookcase. The girl read too many romance novels. No wonder she didn't have much sense when it came to boys. After another minute, I found what I was looking for. Last year's Sandy Harbor High yearbook.

I flipped through it, looking for the junior's section, then looked at the G's. And there she was, alongside her cousins.

Mr. Winters was right. She was very pretty. Now I vaguely remembered her when she came dressed as Pat Benatar. She also looked older than her age, and I wondered if she played that up. Maybe she was a teenage vixen and had seduced Todd Spellman. Then I remembered how many people had said Todd was a jerk and decided he had most likely pursued her.

I flipped through the book, looking for candid shots of Amy. She was a cheerleader, so I wasn't disappointed. She had blond hair, fine features, and displayed the prerequisite cheerleader smile in each picture. Except for one. In that one, she was sitting at a table by herself, nose buried in a book. Was it my imagination, or did she look sad? Maybe she was reading a sad book.

I tried to imagine this little wisp of a girl breaking out every window in Todd's house. Alec was right in that he had a lot of large windows. Even if she had a baseball bat, I doubted she could have done it on her own. If she had a boyfriend with a baseball bat, that could explain it, but I didn't see many pictures of her with boys. Only two, and it was a different boy in each picture. They weren't touching, so I doubted either was her boyfriend. Maybe Daddy Rudy didn't allow his princess to date.

That could explain some things.

Chapter Sixteen

"HI, AMY, I'M ALLIE McSwain. Do you remember my daughter, Jennifer McSwain from last year?" I asked, holding my hand out to shake hers. The poor thing had a deer-in-the-headlights look. I may have startled her when I ran to catch up with her. Lucy had been driving us down Center Street, and I saw her walking toward Fancy Pants, one of Sandy Harbor's dress shops.

She stuck her hand out automatically, and I shook it.

"Sorry for startling you. My daughter Jennifer and I were just looking at her yearbook last night, reliving her senior year, and she saw a picture of you. She mentioned how sweet you were," I said, thinking fast.

"She did?" she asked with a puzzled look on her face.

"Yes, she did. She said you were the best cheerleader Sandy Harbor High has," I said. I was laying it on thick, and I hoped it worked. I needed to ask the girl some questions.

"Hey, Allie, wait up," Lucy called, trotting through the snow-covered sidewalk to catch up. Lucy had gone to park the car after letting me out, and I knew she didn't want to miss anything.

"Oh, there's my friend Lucy. Lucy, this is Amy. Amy, Lucy," I said. I was aware that I probably sounded a little insane and reminded myself to tone it down.

Amy's brow furrowed. "I really have to be going. My mom's expecting me to get home as soon as I find a dress for the winter formal," she said, heading into the shop.

"Hey, Amy, sorry again if I startled you," I said, following her into the shop. "I wondered if I could ask you a question?"

"Sure," she said, glancing at me. "Oh, I remember you. You were at the Halloween party last year, and you brought all those cupcakes to the cheerleader meeting that one time. The little pompom frosting was cute!" She gave me a genuine smile now.

"Yes, I did. I had so much fun making those cupcakes," I said. "So you're looking for a dress for winter formal? Jennifer found the cutest royal blue and silver dress here to wear to her winter formal last year. Oh, look at these dresses." I pointed to a rack that was close to a corner of the store. There were only two other people in the shop, but I didn't want anyone to overhear our conversation. We all headed over to a rack of formal dresses. I glanced over my shoulder, but no one seemed to be paying us any attention.

"These are cute," Lucy said, pulling a purple dress off the rack.

"I like that," Amy said, touching the taffeta.

"Do you have a date for the dance?" I asked. Why wasn't she dress shopping with her mother?

"No. My dad won't let me date," she said, and then looked around the shop. "But I'm meeting Brian Jones at the dance." She smiled without looking at me.

"Well, your secret's safe with us. Listen, Amy, I have a question. Did you know Todd Spellman?"

Her face clouded over, and she looked away. That gave me my answer.

"No," she said and started sliding hangers over, looking through the rack of dresses.

"Are you sure?" I asked.

She turned toward me, her face red with emotion. "He was a dirty old man," she hissed. "He would park across from the school and watch me come out when school was over."

"How did you meet him?" Lucy asked gently.

"He came into my dad's shop to buy plumbing parts. I work there a few hours on Saturdays, and he kept asking me questions. I didn't really think anything of it at first. He seemed really nice. He was friendly."

"Did you tell your dad?" I asked.

"Not at first. I didn't even think about it. But then he started following me home, and no one is at my house in the afternoon. It scared me."

"I don't blame you. I would be scared too," I said. "What did he do?"

Her face clouded over again. "I told him to go away, or I'd tell my dad. He did stop for a while. But then he came back. One day he came to my door and asked to come in. I told him, no, and he put his foot in the door so I couldn't close it. I've never been so scared before."

This was a picture of himself that Todd had hidden from most people. "What happened?" I asked.

"My dad came home. I don't know why. He never comes home before he closes the shop in the evening. If he had been a few minutes later, I don't know what might have happened," she said. Her voice cracked when she said it, and I thought she was going to cry. I was pretty sure I'd cry with her.

"What did your dad do?" Lucy asked. She lowered her voice when the middle-aged woman working in the shop approached.

"Is there anything I can help you ladies with?" she asked. Her voice was shrill and the happiness in it sounded forced.

"No thanks, we're just looking," I said, sounding just as fake as she did.

"All right, let me know if I can help you with anything," she said and wandered off.

Amy looked at me. "My dad got mad. Really mad. He asked him what he was doing there, and when Mr. Spellman said he had rung the wrong doorbell, my dad got mad. He knew he was lying. He threatened him and told him he better not ever come around me again."

"Did he stop?" I asked.

"For a while. But then he started up again. He kept sending me friend requests on Facebook, so I blocked him. But then he made fake profiles, pretending to be girls from my school. I told my dad, and then he didn't bother me again for about a month."

"Wow," I said. "I had no idea he was crazy like that."

Tears formed in Amy's eyes. "He tried to hurt me," she said, her voice cracking. "I was at a football game and he was under the bleachers. I walked by on my way to the restroom, and he jumped out and grabbed me and pulled me under the bleachers."

"Oh, my gosh, what happened?" I asked, afraid of what the answer would be.

"I fought with him. I scratched him and hit him, and then I screamed for help when he took his hand away from my mouth. Then I ran."

"Did you tell anyone? The police? Or your dad?" Lucy asked.

She shook her head. "No, I didn't want anyone to know."

"Oh, Amy, you shouldn't be afraid to tell about something like that," I said. I could feel tears forming in my eyes, and I blinked them back.

"You don't know my dad. He can get so mad. I was afraid of what he would do," she said and wiped her eyes with the back of her hand.

I put a hand on her shoulder and gave it a squeeze. "Amy, don't ever be afraid to tell when someone is hurting you. Please. You need to let someone know."

She looked at the floor and didn't answer me.

I put my arm around her shoulder and hugged her. "I'm going to give you my phone number. Will you call me if you ever need anything? Even if it's just to talk?"

She nodded, and I got a piece of paper from my purse and wrote my phone number down. "Program that into your phone. Please don't hesitate to call me, okay?"

She nodded, but I doubted that she would. She was one of those quiet, shy girls, in spite of being a cheerleader.

I needed to talk to Alec. I would get a lecture, but he needed to know. This would explain the scratches and bruises on Todd's face and chest. It also might explain who killed him if Amy's dad had as bad a temper as she said he did. And I believed her.

Chapter Seventeen

I SAW ALEC DRIVING down Maine Street, and I followed him. I had a hunch as to where he was going, and I was right. He pulled into a parking spot at RG Plumbing Supply, and I pulled into the parking spot next to his.

"Allie?" he said when he got out of his car.

"Hey, Alec, fancy meeting you here," I said with a big smile. "I didn't expect to see you here."

He sighed loudly. "Really? It's such a mystery to you, is it?"

"Uh-huh," I said and closed my car door. "I have a leaky faucet, and I need to see if Rudy has thingamajigs to fix it."

He shook his head at me, but he had a smile on his face.

"Hey," I said, hurrying over to his side, and whispering. "Rudy's daughter is a cheerleader at the high school, and I happened to run into her yesterday afternoon. Todd Spellman was a real class A creep. He had a thing for her and was stalking her. She said he grabbed her under the bleachers at a football game, and they struggled. That explains the scratches and bruises on Todd's face and neck."

Alec leaned back against his car deep in thought. "Do you think she was capable of murdering Todd?"

"Not really. I could be wrong, but she's a tiny little girl, and fairly timid. I always thought of cheerleaders as being self-confident, but she doesn't seem to be. She did say that her father has a pretty nasty temper, and he knew Todd was stalking her."

"There weren't any police reports concerning Todd Spellman in the system. Could be her father decided to handle it on his own," he said.

"Exactly," I said. "But to be honest, if he did do it, I think you should let him go."

He looked at me, wide-eyed. "What do you mean?"

I shrugged. "He did the community a favor. A teenage girl stalker and all-around jerk? I'm not usually in favor of murder, but good riddance."

"I never would have expected to hear that coming out of your mouth, Allie McSwain."

Now I felt bad. "Sorry. I guess that is horrible. But the murder has already been committed. If you said someone was going to go and murder a teenage girl stalker and all-around jerk, I'd say arrest that stalker and all-around jerk, and save someone from committing murder. But the murder has already been committed, and I guess I feel like he deserved it. Does that make me a bad person?"

He shook his head. "No, I think that makes you one of millions that would feel that way. I try not to take anything criminals do personally. It's easier if you don't have an opinion, and you just do your job and arrest the bad guy. Todd may have been a bad guy. But if Rudy Gallo killed him, so is he."

"Okay. I'll try not to take things personally, but that's hard to do when you have a daughter only a year older than Amy Gallo. Jennifer is a little timid herself, and I guess I was imagining the same thing happening to her."

"Understandable," he said and stood up straight. "Now, why don't you go shop for your thingamajig and I'm going to see if I can have a word with Rudy Gallo."

I headed into the shop, and Alec stayed behind. It was good thinking. I could shop for whatever it was I was looking for, and he would look like he wasn't with me. Which, technically, he wasn't. Maybe I would be able to overhear part of the conversation.

"Good morning, Allie," Rudy said from one of the far aisles. He had a cart stacked with small cardboard boxes, and it looked like he was putting stock away.

"Good morning, Rudy," I called, and went down the aisle next to where he was working. The shelves were high enough that he couldn't see me, and I hoped he would forget I was in there.

"Can I help you find something," he called.

"No, that's okay. I think I got it," I answered.

I heard the bell above the door tinkle, and I knew Alec was here. I just hoped he got what he needed from Rudy.

"Good morning, Rudy Gallo?" I heard him say.

"Yeah, that's me," Rudy answered. I could hear wariness in his voice.

"I'm Detective Blanchard, with the Sandy Harbor Police Department. I need to ask you a few questions."

"What for?" Rudy asked.

"Mr. Gallo, how well did you know Todd Spellman?"

Rudy swore under his breath. "He was a piece of trash."

"I see," Alec said, as calm as always. "Did you have many dealings with him?"

"As few as possible," he answered.

It looked like Rudy wasn't going to volunteer anything. I leaned in closer. The aisle I was in had toilet parts. The dust was thick on some of the items, and I suddenly felt a sneeze coming on. I pinched my nose to stop it.

"Can you be more specific?" Alec asked. I could picture him over there with his notepad and pen in hand, calmly making his notes.

"I tried to take out a loan to buy a new house. He said he recommended that I not get the loan. I asked him why, and he said he didn't think I should have a new house."

"Why did he say that?" Alec asked, sounding surprised.

"How should I know? That guy was nuts," Rudy said.

"And this made you angry?" Alec asked.

"Yeah, it made me angry. Who is he to say whether I should have a new house? My business is the only plumbing business for miles around. Everyone comes here for plumbing parts. I do all right, and I wouldn't have a problem paying for a new house. I went over to the Wells Fargo in Bangor and got approved right away," Rudy said bitterly.

"It seems odd that he would want people to go to some other bank in another town to do their business," Alec observed.

"He was an idiot. I don't know how he ever got to be bank manager," Rudy said. "He should have been fired for the way he treated people, but you know, people like that always manage to get ahead. It doesn't make any sense to me."

"Did you have any other contact with him?" Alec asked without commenting.

"Yeah. Yeah, I did. He had a thing for my little girl. I came home from work one day, and he was at my door. He had his foot in it, so my daughter couldn't close it. He was a piece of work." Rudy was getting louder. I could hear the anger in his voice, and I hoped there weren't any other customers in the store. I hadn't thought to look when I first came in.

"What did you do?"

"I told him if he ever came around my daughter again, I'd kill him," he said angrily. There was a brief pause. "Oh. Now, wait a minute. I didn't mean it like that. Don't you go gettin' any ideas. That was just a figure of speech," he said, trying to soften what he had said.

"And did you have any other encounters with him?" Alec asked, calm as you please.

"No. I kept my distance and told my daughter to do the same. I didn't mean it about killing him," he said sounding a bit worried now.

"I understand. Sometimes things get heated, and things get said that you don't mean. Say, there was a rumor going around town that someone went and busted out all of Todd's windows back in September. You didn't hear anything about that, did you?" Alec asked.

"Wh-what? No! No, I don't know anything about any busted windows. I never heard a thing."

Rudy sounded flustered now, and I thought we knew who had broken Todd's windows. I didn't blame him much.

"I appreciate your cooperation, Mr. Gallo. I'll be in touch," Alec said, and I heard him turn and head for the door.

"Hey! Hey, I didn't do nothin' to that freak!" Rudy called after him.

Alec didn't answer him. I heard the bell over the door tinkle and I knew Alec was gone. Now I had the problem of getting out of there without Rudy realizing I heard the whole thing.

Rudy muttered something and heard his shuffling footsteps receding. I realized he was heading for the storeroom, so I tip-toed toward the front door. I peeked around a display, and the coast was clear, so I made a run for the door and was out of there before Rudy remembered I was there.

Alec was still sitting in his car, so I got in the passenger side and closed the door. "So what do you think?"

"I think there's definitely something there. It looks like the girl was telling the truth, and Rudy does seem to have a temper," he said calmly gazing at the side door of Rudy's shop.

"Sounds like it to me, too," I said. "I think he did it."

"You always think everyone did it," he said, glancing at me.

"We haven't got any other suspects, so it seems like a good guess to me."

"That's true, but I try not to rely too heavily on guesses," he said.

"Where to now?" I asked.

"I am going to interview George Dillard and see if he really hated Todd as much as Jane Marshall said he did," he answered.

"Great! Two interrogations in one day," I said.

"And you can't come along," he said.

"Awe," I said, crestfallen. "Oh, but you know, I do need to get some Pepsi," I said brightening. "I heard it's on sale at the Gas and Go."

Alec sighed and refused to look at me. I got out of his car and got into mine.

Chapter Eighteen

THE GAS AND GO'S GAS tanks were roped off in yellow caution tape, and a big moving truck was parked in front of the store. It looked like George Dillard hadn't been able to get a loan to fix them after all. I usually bought gas at the station on Cypress, and I hadn't been over on this side of town in a while.

I parked on the far side of the building, and Alec followed me over and parked beside me.

"Doesn't look good," I said, getting out of my car.

"Sure doesn't," he agreed, and we walked into the store together.

It was shocking to see almost empty shelves. A handful of people milled about, picking through the leftovers.

"Why are all the cans dented?" a little old lady asked, holding up a can of peaches with its side nearly caved in.

"That's the way it came," replied the freckled face kid that was leaning on the register. He didn't look old enough to be out of school and working, and I wondered if he was George's kid.

"I don't think that's true," the older lady muttered, and put the can back on the shelf.

I spotted George leaning against a wall, watching a man in a Pepsi uniform unplug a Pepsi cooler.

I nodded at Alec and motioned toward George.

Alec headed over. "Mr. Dillard?" he asked. I followed along behind him, hoping I wouldn't be noticed and told not to come along.

George looked at him, assessing. "Ayup," he finally said.

"Mr. Dillard, I'm Detective Blanchard, may I have a few words with you?"

George shrugged, but still leaned against the wall. I stepped forward. "George, I didn't know you were going out of business."

Alec glanced at me, but didn't say anything.

He snorted. "Neither did I. But apparently when you don't pass inspection, and your tanks are leaking, you lose your license to sell gas. Without tanks, there isn't much point in a gas station."

"Oh, I'm sorry. I hate to hear it," I said. I knew George from around town. I really couldn't remember when the first time was that I had met him.

Alec stepped closer. People wandered the aisles, searching for something of value to buy for little to nothing.

"Mr. Dillard, did you know Todd Spellman?" Alec asked, lowering his voice.

At the mention of Todd's name, George swore up a blue streak and then spit on the floor. Todd seemed to have that effect on people.

"Yeah, I knew him. And if you ask me, he got what he had comin'. This town is better off without him," he said.

The Pepsi man suddenly got in a hurry to put the cooler on his hand truck and get it out of the store. He nearly hit a store shelf on his way out.

Alec had the notebook out. "Those are rather strong words, Mr. Dillard. Would you care to elaborate on why you feel that way?"

"Oh, come on! Everyone knows Todd Spellman was a backstabber. He would come on all friendly to you and tell you to come down and get a loan to expand your business. Then, he goes and tells the loan department at the bank not to give you the loan." George's face had quickly turned a bright shade of red, and I could see why Jane Marshall had been concerned that he might have a stroke when he had gotten into an argument with Todd at the bank.

"I see. Mr. Dillard, did you ever see Todd Spellman on a personal basis? Did you ever go to his home?" Alec asked, scribbling in his notebook and not looking up at him.

"Oh, yeah, sure. He had a barbecue for business owners a while back. He kept talking up all the good deeds he did. Always talking about charitable contributions he was making. Then he tried to get everyone to give him money for some charity he was starting up. Had the nerve to ask for one thousand dollars from everyone in the room." He snorted. "The guy was crazy."

"What kind of charity?" I asked. I knew Todd had been involved in all sorts of civic endeavors and had even organized a March of Dimes Walk several years ago, but that was all I was aware of.

"Oh, he had some highfalutin name for it. Something like Peace Keepers of Maine or something stupid like that. He planned to raise all this money, and then distribute it to different charities. He planned to get local business owners to donate, and then he would advertise the business owners that did. That way people would be more inclined to shop at our businesses. But if you wanted to be included, you had to give big regularly," he said and laughed bitterly. "Distribute it. Sure, that's how he paid for that new BMW!"

I glanced at Alec. Todd had bought a new BMW several weeks before he died. It looked like it was top of the line, and I had wondered if the bank paid its managers that well the first time I saw it. I hadn't given it another thought after that.

"Did many business owners decide to contribute?" Alec asked.

George shrugged. "I don't know. Some of them weren't too happy about what he was asking for. One thousand to start it off, then five hundred a month to stay included. I said no thanks. Then I had the inspection and went for the loan, and I was turned down. It doesn't take a genius to know why."

"Why didn't you go to another bank and get a loan?" I asked.

He sighed heavily. "Because. My credit isn't great. I already had one loan on the business, and I was late on a couple of payments. Maybe a few. But I tell you, it ain't right to extort money and tell people it's for charity and spend it on yourself."

"Mr. Dillard, do you have anything to add as far as Todd Spellman's death? Maybe you've heard something around town?" Alec asked.

He shook his head. "No. But whoever done it, done us all a favor."

Alec watched him for a few moments, thinking. "It's rumored that someone broke out all of Todd Spellman's windows in his house. You wouldn't happen to know who did that, would you?"

George smiled big. "Are you asking if I did it? No. I didn't do it. But if I had known someone was going over there to do it, I would have gladly gone along to help."

"All right, thank you for your time," Alec said. "I'll be in touch."

"Sorry for your trouble, George," I said as I turned to leave.

"Ah, it ain't nothin'. I'll pick up and start over somewhere else. I guess with my track record with money, it was bound to happen."

"I'm sorry just the same," I said and followed Alec out.

We leaned up against my car, out of sight of the store windows. "Well, he didn't hold anything back," I said.

"It doesn't appear that he did. Right now, it looks like we've got two people that had the motive to kill Todd Spellman," he said thoughtfully.

"I still have to wonder about that phone call that I got from Todd's phone. Connie wasn't very friendly when I brought cookies to her. It just makes me wonder," I said.

"Connie Sutton didn't want your cookies?" Alec asked, one eyebrow cocked.

"I don't know what her problem was. I was just being neighborly. They had a bunch of boxes with paperwork lying around the living room."

"Well, I would imagine they have a lot to sort through," he said, being pragmatic again.

"I guess so," I relented. "What's next?"

"What's next is that you are going to stay out of trouble," he said.

"Hey, what about checking at the lumber yard to see if anyone bought lumber for a deer stand?" I asked.

He chuckled. "It's deer season. How many people do you think have done that and actually went hunting deer and not people? And besides, the lumber was old."

"Sorry, I forgot. I guess it's pointless to see how many deer rifles were sold then?" I said, already knowing the answer.

"I would imagine so," he said and went around to the driver's side door of his car to leave.

"Oh, I almost forgot. We're having dinner at Lucy's tonight at six. Pick me up?"

"Sure," he said. "Sounds like a plan."

Chapter Nineteen

ALEC HAD ONE HAND ON the steering wheel and one hand in mine as we drove over to Lucy's. I had thought I would never be this happy again. It had been such a short time since we met, but I felt as if we had always known each other.

"You know what I want to do for Christmas?" I asked him.

"What?"

"Take a trip to Alabama to introduce you to my mama," I said, turning to him. I fought back the thoughts that said I was rushing things. I wasn't. And I knew it.

"Really?" he asked, glancing at me.

"Yes. Really. We'll take the kids. It's been a couple of years since Thad has gone. I'll show you the kitchen where my grandmama taught me to bake pies and the lake where my older brother taught me to fish."

He smiled, eyes on the road. "That sounds like fun."

"I think you'll like it there. We'll have to teach you to say y'all," I said.

"Well, I can't wait for that," he said. "And why is it that you always say your grandmama taught you to bake pies and not your mother? Certainly, she must have taught you some of what you know."

"Nope. Not a thing. Well, I take that back," I said. "She did teach me to catch lightning bugs and put them in a jar. That's important, you know."

He chuckled. "Indeed, it is. But why didn't she teach you to bake?"

"Because she couldn't. Now and then she would give it a try, but her crust always came out hard as concrete, and her fillings were usually mush. One time she tried to make a lemon meringue pie, and she put so much cornstarch in it the filling had a texture similar to rubber. She couldn't get the egg whites stiff enough to make a meringue, so she skipped that part. It was probably safer for all of us that way."

"So, don't let your mother make Christmas dinner?" he asked.

"No. She can cook better than anyone I know. It's the baking she never was able to master. Grandmama said the baking gene had skipped her and was passed right on down to me."

"Well, I have to agree. You did get the baking gene. Even with all the running I've been doing, I've still managed to gain four pounds in the past month. Can't you make fat free pies?" he asked, pulling into Lucy's driveway.

"Bite your tongue. That's an abomination."

"I'm sure it is," he said and chuckled.

He parked the car, and we headed to the front door. It had rained earlier in the day, and Lucy's front yard was a mess with all the mud. But the rain had brought warmer temperatures, and I was enjoying it.

"Hey, there you guys are," Lucy said, opening the door for us. Her house was warm and cozy. She had spent most of her paychecks on cute decorative items from the flower shop where she worked. Scented candles were placed in every nook and cranny, and floral arrangements adorned nearly every flat surface. Diana Bowen had helped her to decorate before she had been murdered, and I regretted not having her come to my house to help me.

"Hi, Ed, how are you doing?" I asked Lucy's husband. He sat on the sofa, with a football game on the television.

He looked up from the game, his ample body spread out on the sofa. "Hello, Allie. It's good to see you. Alec, would you like a drink?"

"No, thank you. I'm driving. Who's winning?" he asked, nodding at the television.

He shrugged. "I don't know. I never watch football, but Lucy tells me it's un-American not to, so I thought I'd try it."

Alec glanced at me, and I gave him a slight shrug of my shoulders. Ed was one of a kind. You never knew what was going to come out of his mouth.

"Dinner's almost ready," Lucy said as we all took a seat in the living room. "I made roast chicken."

"It smells wonderful," I said.

"So Alec, tell me, did you ever find out who killed Todd Spellman?" Ed asked.

"No, we're still investigating," Alec answered, and reached for a pretzel in a bowl on the coffee table.

"Well, it doesn't really matter. That Todd Spellman was one of the most hated people in town. He had it coming," Ed said matter-of-factly.

"Wait, how do you know that?" Lucy asked.

"That he had it coming or that he was hated?" He shrugged. "I thought everyone knew that. He swindled a bunch of people seven or eight years ago when he started up his own investment company. He sold IRAs and invested them in places that a lot of people thought were just plain foolish. He got away with it though. One thing he did know how to do was cover himself."

"Why have you never mentioned this?" Lucy asked, wide-eyed. I had never heard any of this before, so I was pretty wide-eyed about it, too.

"Like I said, I thought everyone knew. A group of people went to a lawyer to see if they could sue, but the lawyer looked over the paperwork and said there wasn't anything that could be done."

"Well, it seems like you might have mentioned it when you knew Todd had been murdered," Lucy said. She was starting to get cross with him, and I hoped they didn't start arguing.

"Who lost money?" Alec spoke up.

"Well, if I remember, Sam Bailey, Diana Bowen, Rudy Gallo, oh, and his own sister," Ed said. "I don't know who else, but it was a lot of people. He made promises he couldn't keep. I heard no one really invested large amounts, but still. Who has so much money that they don't mind losing some of it?"

"Sam Bailey? The chief of police?" Alec asked.

"The one and only," Ed said.

Alec looked at me.

"Wow," I said.

"Wow is right," he replied.

"I wonder why I hadn't heard about it?" I asked.

"Eight years ago? Sounds like it was right around the time your husband passed away," Lucy pointed out.

"Ah. I wasn't aware of much for a long time after that," I said.

I could only imagine what Alec was thinking right then. He got quiet and didn't say much else, and within a few minutes, Ed and he got interested in the game.

"I think dinner is about ready," Lucy said, and we went into the kitchen to get it ready to be served.

"Sorry about Ed," she said when we were alone. "I don't know about him sometimes. You would have thought he would have mentioned something about Todd being the most hated person in town when he was murdered."

"It must have slipped his mind or something. I have to say, Todd certainly has turned out to be a surprise to me."

"You can say that again," she said.

I hoped Alec figured out who was Todd's murderer soon. The deeper we dug, the more dirt we found.

Chapter Twenty

THE WARMER TEMPERATURES were sticking around, and Alec and I decided we needed to take advantage of it by running outside while we could. The sun was out, and it felt good to be outside, stretching my legs and breathing in the clean air.

We had gone five miles and were near the end of the running trail when I heard it. It was a whistling sound, and I had a flashback to the Turkey Trot. I screamed and hit the ground. I felt the cold mud as my body landed, and it flew up in my face.

Alec looked over his shoulder, wide-eyed.

"What's wrong?" he asked, running to my side.

Then I heard it again, and something hit the mud on the side of the trail, and it flew into the air.

"Get up, Allie! Get up and run!" Alec shouted. He grabbed my arm, jerking me to my feet. The whistling sound came again, and I heard it hit the ground somewhere close.

"Alec," I managed to get out.

"Come on, run!" he said, still holding on to my arm. He pulled me toward some trees, and I heard more whistling sounds, and tree bark flew off a nearby tree.

There was a large, round oak tree, and we hid behind it. Alec was dialing his phone and carefully looking around the tree.

"This is Detective Blanchard, we need backup near the five-mile marker of the running trail. Shots fired. Repeat, shots fired."

He hung up and peered around the tree again.

"Don't do that!" I cried, pulling him back.

"I need to see if I can spot him," he said and leaned forward again.

We were both breathing hard, and my heart felt like it would explode. We were five miles away from Alec's car and gun. The trail ran to the outskirts of town, so there no houses or businesses nearby.

"What do we do?" I whispered and began crying.

"Shh," he said without looking at me.

I heard sirens in the distance and whispered a prayer of thanks. I hoped they got here in time. There was silence around us, but I didn't think the shooter was gone. I hoped he wouldn't pop up on the other side of us and shoot us both dead.

"Get down," Alec said.

I crouched down low, making sure I stayed behind the safety of the tree.

"I'm going to run to that other tree over there. I want you to sit tight. Don't move."

"No!" I whispered, but he wouldn't listen. He ran and hid behind the other tree. I wanted to look and see if I could see anyone, but I didn't want to become a target. I was too terrified to move.

The sirens were getting closer, but they still sounded so far away. Would they get here in time? My breathing came out raw and jagged. I put my hand on my chest and could feel my heart pounding. Taking deep breaths wasn't helping it slow down.

I finally leaned around the tree a little to see Alec better. Just as I did, he ran to another tree. I wasn't sure if he saw something or was still trying to figure out where the shooter was.

We were sitting ducks. Why hadn't I insisted he wear his gun? It would have looked ridiculous, but at this point, I didn't care.

It felt like forever, but four police cars finally arrived. The police officers jumped out with guns drawn. Yancey Tucker ran to where I was crouching. I could hear his breathing coming hard and fast.

"Are you okay, Allie?" he asked, visually scanning the area.

"Yeah, I'm okay," I said and started crying again. "Someone was shooting at us. They had a silencer just like when Todd was shot."

"Come on, we're going to run back to my car and you're going to get inside and get low on the seat, okay?"

"Okay," I whispered.

"Ready? Run!" he said, and we both ran to his car, with him behind me.

I jumped in the backseat, and he closed the door. I lay on the seat, sobbing and shaking and hoping Alec was okay. I listened for more gunshots, but none came.

I lay there for what seemed forever when the car door opened. When I looked up, Alec hovered over me.

"Oh my God," I said and jumped into his arms.

"It's okay. Everything's okay," he soothed.

I sobbed in his arms for a few minutes, just thankful we were both okay. "Did you find them?" I asked, pulling away to look into his face.

He shook his head. "No. I'm sure they ran as soon as they realized I had called for backup. They're gone. Yancey is going to drive us back to my car."

We sat in silence, holding hands in the backseat, during the short drive to his car. "Okay?"

I nodded. We got out of the police cruiser and got into Alec's car. I looked around, making sure the shooter wasn't near. Alec waved to Yancey as he drove off.

"Oh, Alec, I don't know what I would have done if you had been hurt," I said, turning toward him. "You shouldn't have run over to that other tree."

He gave me a small grin. "I've had a little experience in this kind of thing. We're okay. That's all that matters."

"I know you know what you're doing, but you scared me!"

"I'm sorry. We're safe now."

He pulled into my driveway and parked.

"I can't believe that just happened," I said.

"I know. I'm sorry you were involved in this," he said softly.

I turned to look at him. "We could have died."

"But we didn't. We need to focus on that, Allie."

"You're right. I know."

We got out of his car and went inside my house. The killer knew who we were, and they wanted us stopped. And that meant we were getting close.

Chapter Twenty-One

"WHERE ARE WE GOING?" Lucy asked as we drove down Center Street.

"I don't know," I said. And I didn't. I had tossed and turned all night long. Someone wanted Alec and me dead. The facts of the case turned circles in my head. I had finally drifted off to sleep around three in the morning when I heard that whistling sound go right past my ear. I sat up screaming, with the darkness of the room closing in on me. It took a few seconds to realize that I had imagined it. I had gotten up and made myself some coffee and didn't go back to bed. I was paying for it now. I could hardly keep my swollen eyes open.

"Hey," she said, putting her hand on the back of mine. "It's going to be okay. Alec will find the killer."

"I know. It's just hit really close to home is all," I said.

"If you want, you can come and stay in my spare bedroom. It might make you feel better."

"Thanks. I'll think about it," I said. The truth was, I wasn't sure if I wanted to be around other people. An odd, depression-like state had come over me. It felt a little like what I went through when my husband had died. I suddenly wanted to be alone, and I wasn't sure why.

"Drink your coffee before it gets cold," she admonished, motioning toward the cup holder.

"I think I'm all coffeed out. I've drunk more today than I have in the past month," I said. "Hey, turn down Main."

She did, driving slowly on the narrow street. It had turned cold overnight, and the roads were icy. There was a dark blue pickup parked on the street in front of Rudy's shop. The license plate said RG PLMG.

"Stop the car," I said.

"What?" Lucy asked, glancing at me, wide-eyed.

"Park the car, I want to talk to Rudy Gallo."

She did as I asked, pulling into the parking spot next to the blue truck. I jumped out of the car and hurried into the plumbing store. Rudy was standing at the register, just finishing up with a customer. I strode over to him as the customer picked up his bag of plumbing parts.

"How could you?" I exclaimed, looking at Rudy.

"What?" he asked, looking puzzled.

"I know what you did!" I accused. "You aren't going to get away with this."

"What are you talking about, Allie?" Rudy asked. He glanced at the customer but got no help from him as he scurried out the door.

"I know what you did," I repeated.

Rudy shook his head. "I don't know what you're talking about!"

"You tried to kill Alec and me yesterday," I said through clenched teeth. My depression had turned to rage. There was no way he was going to get away with this.

"What are you talking about?" he asked. "Are you out of your mind? I have no idea what you're talking about."

"You shot at us while we were on the running trail," I seethed. "You killed Todd Spellman. You're a murderer!"

The door swung open, the little bell above it tinkling, and Lucy entered the shop.

"Allie, that's not true, I did not kill Todd Spellman, and I certainly didn't shoot at you or Alec. What's wrong with you?" Rudy asked.

"Allie?" Lucy whispered.

I turned to look at her, and she looked at me wide-eyed.

"He killed Todd," I explained more calmly than I felt.

"Honey, why don't we go home now? You're tired," Lucy said gently.

"You better get her out of here. She's off her rocker," Rudy said. "I don't know what's gotten into her."

I turned back to Rudy. "That's your truck out front. I saw the rifle rack you have in it. I know you killed Todd Spellman, and you tried to kill Alec and me. You aren't going to get away with it." I could hear the desperation in my own voice. Thoughts swirled around my mind. He had done it, hadn't he? He had all the reason in the world to do it. He was protecting his daughter by killing Todd, and he was afraid that Alec and I had figured it out.

He narrowed his eyes at me. "I haven't hunted in years. I just never took that rack out. What does that have to do with anything?" Rudy asked. He turned to Lucy. "Get her out of here before I call the cops."

"Come on, Allie," Lucy said gently. "Let's get you home." She approached me cautiously and took my hand.

I looked from Rudy to Lucy. They were looking at me as if I were some kind of monster. "You believe me, don't you?" I pleaded with Lucy. Couldn't she see the truth of what had happened?

"I'm callin' the cops," Rudy warned.

Lucy raised a hand to him. "Just hold on."

"Call whoever you want," I said through gritted teeth. "You're not going to get away with this!"

She glanced at Rudy and then back to me. "Let's go home and talk about it. I'll call Alec, and we'll talk. Rudy isn't going anywhere. Alec will talk to him if he thinks he should."

I stared at Rudy, and the silence surrounding me roared in my ears. *What am I doing?*

"Come on, Allie, let's go," Lucy said calmly when I didn't move.

I let her lead me to the door and took one last look at Rudy. All I could see was confusion on his face.

"Sorry," Lucy said to Rudy as the bell above the door tinkled, and then the door closed behind us.

"Here, get in the car," she said, opening the passenger side door for me.

I got in and stared off into space. Then I broke down sobbing. I needed sleep. Lots and lots of sleep. And I needed Alec. I needed him to talk some sense into me.

Chapter Twenty-Two

SUNLIGHT STREAMED THROUGH my window as I struggled to regain consciousness. The events of the past two days came flooding back as I forced my eyes open. I felt a wave of humiliation wash over me as I remembered what happened at Rudy Gallo's store. What had I done?

I reached across the bed and felt Alec, asleep next to me. I had taken a sleeping pill the night before but still had had problems going to sleep. He had insisted on staying the night with me, sleeping on top of the blankets, still in his clothes. I pushed back the layer of heavy blankets and struggled to get free of them. After a few moments of fighting the sheets, I was free. Alec slept on, exhausted from trying to calm me. I was fuzzy on the details, but I thought we had fallen asleep sometime after two in the morning, with the TV volume turned low to help lull me to sleep.

I stumbled to the kitchen, tripping over my cat, Dixie. He meowed and scurried out of my way.

"Sorry," I mumbled and hit the corner of the kitchen counter with my side.

I started the coffee and opened the blinds in the kitchen to let light stream in. The tile floor of the kitchen was cold, and I wished I had put my slippers on but I was too tired to make the trip back to the bedroom to put them on.

Just as I was pouring a cup of coffee, the phone on the wall rang. I jumped, spilling the coffee onto the counter, and stared at the phone. After three rings, I set the coffee pot and my cup down and staggered over to stand in front of the phone.

Todd Spellman.

"Stop it," I whispered as it rang on. Four times, five times, six times.

On the eighth ring, I picked up the receiver and listened. There was a long period of silence while I listened, having forgotten to say hello. I began to wonder if it had even rung. and I started to hang up the receiver, and then, there was a weak "hello."

I gasped and put the receiver back to my ear. "Hello?" I whispered.

"Hello," the voice said again.

"Hello," I repeated. Then silence again. "Who is this?"

"Is this Allie?" the fragile voice asked.

"Yes, who is this?" I asked.

"Earl Spellman," the voice said.

I searched my memory. Did I know an Earl Spellman? I knew Todd, but he was dead. Maybe he had other relatives in town for the funeral? Then I realized it might be Mr. Spellman. I couldn't recall ever hearing his first name.

"Mr. Spellman?" I asked. "Todd Spellman's father?"

"Yes," the voice creaked out. "I wanted to tell you something. Something bad."

My heart pounded in my chest, and I checked the kitchen clock as if that would ground me in reality.

"What?" I whispered.

"Killers are in my house," he said.

The room began to spin, and everything went black. *Killers?*

When I came back to myself, I was still standing with the receiver to my ear, and I was staring at the phone on the wall.

"Allie?" Alec said gently.

I turned and looked at him. Then I glanced at the clock. Ten minutes had passed.

"We need to get to the Spellman's. Now," I said, and reached to put the receiver in its cradle, and fumbled it, almost dropping it. I made another try, and it landed safely in the cradle.

"Why do we need to do that?" he asked gently.

"The killers are there. We need to go now," I said, turning toward him. "Now."

"Allie, maybe we need to rest today. You know, just take it easy," he said. He had dark circles under his eyes, and his hair stood up on the back of his head from where he had lain on it. The creases in his clothes were a mix of deep and small.

"We have to protect Mr. Spellman," I said, feeling desperation coming on. "Now."

I headed toward my bedroom to change my clothes. I had slept in warm flannel pajamas, and I still had enough of my wits about me to know I couldn't go out in public that way. I stumbled, feeling drunk from the sleeping pill, but got to my bedroom just the same.

"Allie, please," Alec said, following me.

I grabbed a sweatshirt and jeans and went into the bathroom to change. "Alec, if you've ever believed or trusted me about anything, you have to believe me about this," I said through the closed door. I hurriedly took my pajamas off and got dressed.

"Allie, I'm not sure we should do this. I think we both need more sleep," he said.

"Alec, I am going with or without you," I said, catching up my hair and putting a hair tie on it to hold it in check.

"Allie," he started when I opened the door.

"Alec," I said and looked at him. "Mr. Spellman called, and he said the killers are there in the house with him."

Alec stared at me and moment, and then said, "Okay. But you let me do the talking. I want you to stay calm and in control, is that understood?"

"Yes. Bring your gun."

Chapter Twenty-Three

I STUMBLED WHEN I GOT out of the car but regained my balance before I took a spill. I needed to get a grip.

"Okay?" Alec asked, concerned.

"Yeah," I said, and we headed to the front door.

"Why don't you stay in the car?" Alec whispered and took hold of my arm.

"I got this. You got your gun?" I asked.

"Yes. You promised you would stay quiet," he reminded me.

"Got it," I said and rang the doorbell.

Sounds of people moving about inside could be heard through the door. I hoped we weren't too late. When no one came to the door right away, I rang the doorbell again.

The door swung open, and Terrence stood looking at us, wide-eyed. After a moment, he narrowed his eyes at me. "What are you doing here at this hour? It's too early for visitors."

"Excuse the intrusion," Alec said, smiling. "We'd like to speak with Mr. Spellman if that's all right."

"He's still sleeping," he said. "I think we've given you all the information you need. There isn't anything else to tell you."

Alec still had a smile on his face when he said, "Yes, you've certainly been cooperative in this investigation, but I'd like to remind you that the investigation is ongoing." Only a fool would think he didn't mean business, smile or no smile.

Terrence considered this for a few moments, then opened the door wide and led us into the living room. "What is it you need to know? Maybe I can supply the information you need," he said over his shoulder.

"What's going on?" Connie asked from the kitchen. I could smell biscuits baking, and I was suddenly hungry.

"The detective, and uh, Ms. McSwain need more information," Terrence said dryly.

Connie went pale. She turned away and left the kitchen without another word. I wanted to follow her, but I knew Alec wouldn't like it.

"I'd like to speak to Mr. Spellman. If he isn't feeling well, that's perfectly understandable. I can go in to speak to him," Alec said to Terrence.

Terrence looked at us, considering. "No, I'll go get him." He left us standing in the living room.

"Maybe you should follow him," I whispered. "He might do something."

"It's okay," Alec said. "Just relax."

But everything inside me was saying not to relax. Every nerve in my body was standing at attention.

After we had waited for what seemed forever, Terrence came back to the living room, pushing Mr. Spellman in his wheelchair. There was a blanket over his lap, and he had that glassy-eyed look he had when Todd was alive. "Here he is," Terrence said brightly.

I glanced at Alec. I could see the hesitation in his eyes.

"Good morning, Mr. Spellman," Alec said. "How are you doing?"

Mr. Spellman looked at Alec blankly, drool running down his chin, and then he looked away.

"He doesn't seem well this morning," Alec said to Terrence. "Has he been ill?"

Terrence smiled. "Well, I'm afraid this is as good as it gets with him. For a small space of time, he did seem better after his meds were adjusted, but he's back to his old self. Dementia, you know."

"I see," Alec said and looked at me.

I wanted to scream. I had not dreamed our conversation earlier. Sleep meds or not, I was sure of it. I stepped forward and squatted down in front of Mr. Spellman. "How are you doing, Mr. Spellman?" I asked.

He looked at me and focused his eyes. His mouth opened, and it seemed like he was going to speak, but then he closed it again.

"Are you doing okay?" I asked him.

Mr. Spellman opened his mouth and closed it twice more. "No," he finally squeaked out.

"What's going on?" I asked him in a rush.

"Now look, I can't have the two of you harassing a sickly old man," Terrence objected, taking a step toward me.

"She isn't harassing anyone," Alec said.

"What is it?" I asked Mr. Spellman.

He struggled, opening his mouth and closing it. Then he shook his head, closed his eyes, and leaned his head back.

"There, see? He isn't feeling well. I need to get him back to bed," Terrence said and took hold of the wheelchair handles. Alec put his hand out and stopped him from moving the chair.

"Tell me," I pleaded.

Mr. Spellman suddenly sat up and opened his eyes. He looked at me, then pointing a knobby finger in Terrence's direction and croaked out, "Killer!"

At that, Terrence leaped away from Alec and sprinted for the hall. Alec was faster and more nimble and knocked him down before he got to it. Seconds later, Alec had handcuffs on him.

"Let him go!"

We all looked up, and Connie stood in the hallway with a deer rifle in her hands, pointed at Alec.

"You don't want to do that, Connie," Alec said. "Put the gun down."

"No. We aren't going to jail. I'm going to take my father home with me," she said through trembling lips.

"Connie, put the gun down," Alec said calmly.

"Don't listen to him, Connie," Terrence said. "We'll take your father home with us, just like you said. No one will know what happened here."

"Connie, you don't want to do anything rash. Put the gun down," Alec said. He was still lying on top of Terrence. Terrence started to thrash about and tried to throw him off.

My mind tried to come up with something I could do to help Alec, but Connie had a clear view of me. If I made a move, she would see it and shoot me or Alec, or both of us.

"You put down!" Mr. Spellman croaked out with all the strength he could muster.

Everyone turned toward him, and he pointed a long bony finger at his daughter. "Murderer!"

His indictment brought Connie to tears, and she lowered the rifle. Alec sprang to his feet and took hold of the gun, pulling it from her hands. "Go sit on the sofa," he ordered.

Connie covered her face with one hand and made her way to the sofa. "I'm so sorry, Daddy," she sobbed. "I did it for you. Todd was hurting you, keeping you drugged up like he was."

"No," Mr. Spellman said firmly.

Alec called for backup, and I took a seat on an armchair. I was exhausted.

"I don't know how you could kill your brother," I said in disgust.

"You don't understand!" she wailed. "He was evil. He was spending all of my father's money and keeping him drugged up so he couldn't do anything to stop him."

"Your father loved him. He was his son, and your brother," I pointed out. I should have left well enough alone, but I was still angry about being shot at. Twice. "Then you tried to kill Alec and me."

"You wouldn't leave well enough alone. Those stupid cookies! Why couldn't you leave it alone?" she asked.

"My cookies aren't stupid," I said, bewildered. No one had ever called my cookies stupid.

"Connie, shut up!" Terrence said from the floor. "Just shut up!"

I could hear sirens in the distance, and I leaned back and breathed a sigh of relief.

Chapter Twenty-Four

I SAT ON THE SOFA, wrapped in a blanket, watching old black and white episodes of *I Love Lucy*. It took my mind off things while I waited for Alec. Lucy dozed fitfully on the loveseat, having given up her plan to stay up with me as long as it took for Alec to get things settled down at the police station. It didn't matter. I was relieved the killers had been caught, and no one else had been harmed.

There was a light knock on the front door, and I jumped up to get it. Alec stood on the stoop, knit hat covering his ears. It was a cold but clear night, with millions of stars in the sky.

"Hey," he said.

"Hey," I said. "Come in and warm up."

He followed me back to the living room where Lucy was stirring, and the Lucy on the television was stomping on grapes. Canned laughter filled the room.

"I love *I Love Lucy*," Alec said and sat on the sofa.

"Me too," I said and sat next to him. "So did they tell all?"

"They did. After a little persuasion. They believed Todd was stealing all of his father's money and keeping him drugged. We don't know how true it is about the money yet, but the drugged part seems to be true, because when we saw him at their home, and he was more alert, it was due to a change in his meds, just like they told us."

"Seems like they could have talked to Todd instead of killing him."

He chuckled. "They did. Connie has wanted to bring her father to their home for years now, but Todd refused. So they took things into their own hands."

"Why was he so out of it when we saw him today?" I asked.

"Connie confessed that they caught him making that phone call to you. They didn't hear the whole conversation and didn't know who he had called, but they figured he had said enough to make someone suspicious. They gave him sedatives, and were trying to get out of the house before anyone got there."

"Ah." That made sense.

"Connie said she panicked when she took shots at us at the Turkey Trot. She thought we saw more than we did. Terrence is an ace marksman, and he was the one that shot and killed Todd."

"And who shot at us on the running trail? Connie?" I asked.

He nodded. "Indeed. It seems you irritated her with all your baked goods and stopping by, and she was paranoid that you knew more than you did. So she decided to take care of us before they left the state. Fortunately for us, she's a terrible shot."

I shook my head. "How could someone be irritated with my baked goods?"

Lucy giggled, having just woke up.

"You hush over there," I said.

Alec chuckled and laid his head back against the sofa. "Let's just be thankful she's such a bad shot."

"Well, I guess we can be thankful for that," I said. "I wonder where Mr. Spellman got my phone number. And what will happen to him now?"

"We made some phone calls, and he has a much younger sister in Idaho. She's going to come and pick him up. The drugs they gave him were wearing off, and he said he had an old phone book. Your number was listed, and your name was the only name he could remember, so he called you."

"Huh. Phone book. I forgot those things existed. I Google everyone and everything these days."

"The joys of technology," he said. "I've also made a decision."

"Oh?" I asked.

"Yes. I'm officially retiring from the police department. I've put in thirty years, and I've decided it's enough."

"Wow," Lucy said. "That's something."

"Really? What will you do?" I asked.

"Maybe I'll start a blog," he said thoughtfully. "Or maybe I'll become a private eye. I can set my own hours and decide which cases I want to handle. I can even wear a fedora just like Ricky Ricardo."

I snickered. "That could be fun. Then I don't have to bake cookies for Sam Bailey to keep him from being mean to you, and he can't keep me from going on investigations with you."

"Oh. Well, I hadn't thought of that," he said.

"Yes, I can be your partner! That's a wonderful idea," I said, getting excited.

"Me too," Lucy said. "It will be so much fun!"

"Oh, no," Alec said. "You both have jobs. Remember? You work in a flower shop, Lucy, and you have a blog, Allie. You won't have time to help me."

"Nope, Dick Bowen is selling the flower shop," Lucy said. "I'll be footloose and fancy-free."

"And I've already decided to end the blog. I'll have time on my hands as well," I said.

Alec groaned. "Suddenly the blog idea sounds better than the private eye idea."

"I have leftover blueberry pie in the kitchen. Let's celebrate," I said.

I was glad Alec was going to retire. He didn't seem to like working for Sam Bailey, and it would give him more free time to spend with me. And that was an excellent idea.

THE END

Sneak Peek

Candy Cane Killer
A Freshly Baked Cozy Mystery, book 4
Chapter One

I SIGHED WHEN WE TURNED onto Montrose Street. I was home. My Mama and Daddy had bought the house I grew up in during the first year of their marriage, nearly fifty years ago. Daddy had passed away almost twenty years earlier, but Mama would stay put in that house for the rest of her life, I was sure. The house had all the charm you would expect in an old Southern home.

A white picket fence surrounded the property, and the cottage style house boasted gingerbread trim and a wide wraparound porch. Magnolia trees shaded the front yard and rose bushes lined the white picket fence.

There was a large backyard with peach, apple, plum, and pear trees. The porch was my favorite part of the house. It was wide and accommodating, and Daddy had installed wide paddled ceiling fans so the summers would be more bearable during the evenings. Tears sprang to my eyes as we pulled into the driveway.

"We're home, kids," I said and wiped my eyes with a tissue.

"What a beautiful house," Alec remarked.

"Isn't it?" I said and opened the door to the minivan we had rented at the airport in Mobile. Mama hated to drive far, even though she was only in her early seventies, and I had decided it would just make things easier all the way around if we rented the van.

That way we would also have it to run around town if we wanted to.

The front door swung open, and Mama came out and stood on the porch and waved. I broke into a run and threw myself into her arms and started crying all over again.

How was it I had managed to move so far away and stayed away all these years? Moments like this made me so homesick I thought I would curl into a ball and never stop crying.

"What are you crying about?" Mama murmured into my hair.

"I miss you so much. You need to move to Maine so you'll be closer," I said. It was pointless to say it. Mama was an Alabama girl and an Alabama girl she would stay. I wondered how hard it would be to get Alec to move to Alabama.

"Grandma!" Jennifer said and elbowed me out of the way so she could hug Mama.

I took a step back and turned toward Alec and smiled. He had the back of the minivan open and was getting the luggage out. I went to him as Thad hugged Mama and introduced his new girlfriend, Sarah.

"Hey, I have someone for you to meet," I said.

He smiled at me and took my hand as we headed back for the front porch. Mama had my brother Jake put up clear Christmas lights around the edge of the roof and the porch railing. It was after seven in the evening and dark out, but the house was lit up so that it was a beautiful sight. A larger than life wreath hung on the front door. The wreath was decorated with red glass ball ornaments and red felt Santas.

"Mama, this is Alec," I said.

"Well, pleased to meet you, young man," she said and pushed past his outstretched hand.

"Oh," he said in surprise as she hugged him tightly.

"Pleased to meet you, Mrs. Hamilton."

"Now, don't you call me Mrs. Hamilton. That's far too formal. Allie has told me all about you, and I feel like I know you already. You can call me Mama," she said, taking a step back to look him over. Then she turned to me. "He is a looker, Allie. I must say you do know how to pick 'em."

"Yes, I do!" I agreed and laughed.

Alec went pink beneath the Christmas lights and glanced at me, looking uncomfortable.

"Well, I think I'll get the luggage out," he said and wandered off.

I looked at Mama, and we laughed as he retreated to the van.

Poor Alec. We Southern women were going to get the best of him.

"Let's get inside. It's getting late, and I've made a light supper for y'all," she said and led the way into the house, still chuckling at Alec's embarrassment.

"I'll help Alec with the luggage," Thad said and headed to the van.

Inside, the house was warm and cozy and smelled of roasted ham and sweet potatoes. Mama may have said she had made a light supper, but what that really meant was a small feast. She was incapable of making small amounts of food if she was going to be feeding more than herself.

"Oh, that tree smells wonderful," Sarah said and went over to the large blue spruce standing in the corner. She reached out a hand to touch one of its branches and exclaimed, "It's real!"

"Oh, yes ma'am," Mama said. "I don't believe in plastic Christmas trees. There's no real Christmas spirit in those fake ones."

Each branch was lightly flocked and filled with lights and ornaments. Tiny plastic toys made in the 1950s sat next to delicate German glass balls with glitter and painted scenes on them from the 1940s. Mama had draped long strands of silver tinsel on each branch, giving the tree a shimmering effect. I remembered being given that job as a young girl and being told over and over, to hang one strand at a time on the branches. If it had been up to me, I would have tossed handfuls of the stuff onto the branches and been done with it. Mama wouldn't have it.

In front of each light, she had swirled white gossamer angel hair, giving the tree a dreamy look. I had never had the patience to decorate a tree as she did, but I had to admit, it was worth the time and trouble.

"Wow, I've never had a real tree before," Sarah said. She inhaled deeply. "It smells so fresh!"

"My goodness, child, you've never lived then," Mama said and winked at me. "That's the smell of Christmas."

"No, I haven't," Sarah agreed, looking at the tree wistfully.

"I'm starving, Grandma," Jennifer said, going to the kitchen. "I smell biscuits."

"They'll be done in about two minutes," Mama said, and then turned to me. "Come on into the kitchen."

Mama cooked on an old fashioned stove from the 1940s. I had admired it all my life, with its extra oven and warming bins. I had seen restored stoves similar to hers on Pinterest and eBay and had drooled over a pink one for months. It wouldn't fit the décor of my kitchen, but how I longed for that stove. I thought it might be worth a kitchen remodel to have it.

I heard Alec and Thad stomp up the porch steps and come into the living room. "I'll show you where to put them," I heard Thad say, and they went down the hall.

"So, how serious are you about that man?" Mama leaned toward me and whispered.

I glanced at Jennifer. She had finally settled into the idea of me dating again, but she still wasn't thrilled about it. She had finally admitted she couldn't argue that I hadn't waited long enough after her father had died. Eight years was long enough. But I didn't think she was ready to think about Alec and I doing anything more than dating.

I nodded toward Jennifer, who was checking out the contents of Mama's refrigerator and not paying attention to our conversation.

"Oh," Mama mouthed and smiled real big. "Well, I suggest that everyone get washed up, and we'll get this food on the table."

"Wow, it smells good in here," Alec said, following Thad into the kitchen. "Is there anything I can do to help?"

"You can set yourself down at the table, and Allie and I will have the food set out right quick," Mama said, opening the oven door and pulling out a pan of biscuits.

Alec smiled at me and did as he was told. We had all eaten very sparsely on the plane, and we were starving. There was nothing like home cooking, especially when it was my Mama's home and her cooking.

Mama put the biscuits in a red glass mixing bowl and covered them with a white flour sack dishcloth. I got the ham out and set it on the table, followed by sweet potatoes, green beans, coleslaw, potato salad, strawberry jam, and real butter. It was a feast, and I was going to have to do some serious running if I expected to not gain weight while we were here.

Mama bowed her head and said Grace and we started passing bowls and serving trays.

"I'm so glad y'all were able to come for Christmas. I can hardly believe I get you for two weeks," Mama said.

"We have so been looking forward to this trip," I said, cutting into a slice of ham. She had put cherry jam on the ham as it cooked, and it had caramelized and thickened into a delectable coating.

"This is perfection," I said after taking a bite.

"So, Grandma, how is the Christmas baking going?" Jennifer asked innocently.

"Now, don't you tease me, young lady. You know how it's going. It isn't. However, your Aunt Shelby brought by a banana cream pie for dessert tonight. She was in town this morning. But smart-alecky girls don't get any," she said, buttering a biscuit.

Jennifer snickered. "I don't know of any smart-alecky girls around here, Grandma."

"I can't wait to see Shelby and Jake," I said. I turned to Alec. "You'll love them. They're just like me, only not as good looking." I grinned.

"I have no doubts about that. You do look a good deal like your mother," he said.

"Yes, I do," I agreed. "Everyone has always said that." My mother hadn't aged much in the past twenty years, and I envied that and hoped I would take after her in that regard. Her hair was naturally curly, and she kept it short. The red in it had faded, but it was a pretty color, nonetheless.

"So, what do you kids want to do tomorrow?" Mama asked, looking around the table.

"Sleep in," Thad said. "Please. We flew to Maine in the middle of the night and then got on another plane early this morning."

"Sleep it is," she said. Then she turned to me. "I think we should bake some gingerbread men sometime this week."

"We" meant me, and that was fine. She could handle the decorating duties, and I would bake.

Gingerbread men were a tradition in our family. We used an old recipe called Joe Froggers. Christmas wouldn't be Christmas without Joe Froggers.

When I was a little girl, my grandmama had told me that Joe Froggers were a Southern specialty. When I moved to Maine, I discovered they were actually a Northern specialty, and I hadn't had the heart to tell her. I discovered that a man called Old Black Joe and His wife Aunt Crease had come up with the cookie, using rum to help preserve them in the 1800s in Massachusetts.

They were made into cookies the size of lily pads and were the best gingerbread-type cookie I have ever tasted.

They became the Hamilton family traditional gingerbread cookie, and I couldn't wait to make them.

Buy Candy Cane Killer on Amazon

https://www.amazon.com/ Candy-Cane-Killer-Freshly-Mystery-ebook/dp/ B01MDR3HVB

If you'd like updates on the newest books I'm writing, follow me on Amazon and Facebook:

https://www.facebook.com/ Kathleen-Suzette-Kate-Bell-authors-759206390932120/

https://www.amazon.com/Kathleen-Suzette/e/ B07B7D2S4W/ref=dp_byline_cont_pop_ebooks_1

Made in the USA
Las Vegas, NV
18 March 2025